W9-APG-989

Josie tied the scarf around Trent's eyes

"Is that really necessary?" he asked.

"Absolutely. When vision is impaired, the other senses are heightened. And I told you not to ask questions."

"I thought all teachers liked curious stu—" She cut him off with a soft, slow kiss. And then she was gone. A moment later he heard a slow jazz tune start to play, heard the barely audible fall of her footsteps on the carpet coming back to him. He could see her in his mind, wearing the sexy black lace bustier and garter belt. The image was almost more tantalizing than the real thing.

She unbuttoned his shirt, opened his jeans. Trent let out a soft groan when her hand brushed him.

Her breath tickled his neck, and then she whispered, "Do you like it when I touch you there?"

"Yes," he said, his voice strained. "I do."

She slid her hand down his thigh, and back up, continued up his belly to his chest. She pulled aside his shirt and her hair brushed against him as she trailed kisses up his chest to his neck, her hand once again drifting south, lightly teasing.

Trent gasped and let his head fall back.

"Do you want me to touch you...more?"

Blaze™

Dear Reader,

I once saw a scene on a TV show where the heroine gets even with a guy who had done her wrong by seducing him out of his clothes and then kicking him out of her car before driving away. I thought it was a funny scene, but I couldn't help reimagining it. What if he hadn't done anything to deserve such treatment? What if she had a reason for driving away besides revenge? And what if the two would-be lovers met again a few years later, with their own agendas—his being revenge and hers being seduction?

That is how *Pleasure for Pleasure,* my first Harlequin Blaze novel, was born. I had great fun writing this story of sensual revenge and its many unexpected side effects. And only in Blaze could those side effects be so steamy!

Josie and Trent's story is set in San Francisco—a city of romance and possibilities. San Francisco holds a special place in my heart. My husband proposed to me there, and we've shared many memorable moments in the city since then. I hope Trent and Josie's romance touches you, makes you laugh and inspires you to find your own romantic spot to share with someone special.

I love to hear from readers, so write and tell me what you think of *Pleasure for Pleasure.* You can reach me via my Web site, www.jamiesobrato.com, or you can write to me care of Harlequin Enterprises Ltd., 225 Duncan Mill Road, Don Mills, Ontario M3B 3K9, Canada.

Sincerely,

Jamie Sobrato

Books by Jamie Sobrato

HARLEQUIN TEMPTATION
911—SOME LIKE IT SIZZLING

PLEASURE FOR PLEASURE

Jamie Sobrato

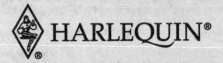

HARLEQUIN®

TORONTO • NEW YORK • LONDON
AMSTERDAM • PARIS • SYDNEY • HAMBURG
STOCKHOLM • ATHENS • TOKYO • MILAN • MADRID
PRAGUE • WARSAW • BUDAPEST • AUCKLAND

If you purchased this book without a cover you should be aware that this book is stolen property. It was reported as "unsold and destroyed" to the publisher, and neither the author nor the publisher has received any payment for this "stripped book."

To my mother, Sherry Bush, for instilling in me a love of reading that grew into a love of writing

ISBN 0-373-79088-0

PLEASURE FOR PLEASURE

Copyright © 2003 by Jamie Sobrato.

All rights reserved. Except for use in any review, the reproduction or utilization of this work in whole or in part in any form by any electronic, mechanical or other means, now known or hereafter invented, including xerography, photocopying and recording, or in any information storage or retrieval system, is forbidden without the written permission of the publisher, Harlequin Enterprises Limited, 225 Duncan Mill Road, Don Mills, Ontario, Canada M3B 3K9.

All characters in this book have no existence outside the imagination of the author and have no relation whatsoever to anyone bearing the same name or names. They are not even distantly inspired by any individual known or unknown to the author, and all incidents are pure invention.

This edition published by arrangement with Harlequin Books S.A.

® and TM are trademarks of the publisher. Trademarks indicated with ® are registered in the United States Patent and Trademark Office, the Canadian Trade Marks Office and in other countries.

Visit us at www.eHarlequin.com

Printed in U.S.A.

1

DOGS...DOLLS...DONUTS...but no Dominatrixes? Josie Marcus flipped through the D section of the Yellow Pages again to make sure she hadn't missed anything, maybe a tiny listing that read, "For Dominatrixes, see Erotic Service Professionals." She scanned the pages more carefully. No, nothing.

Now she had no idea where else to find a last-minute guest speaker on the topic of Introductory S&M. Her scheduled dominatrix had just canceled, leaving her with twenty-four hours to fill a slot, or face dropping yet another seminar from the already spotty schedule. There had been a Rolodex full of phone numbers for past speakers at the Lovers for Life Center, but last week the center's resident cat, Eros, had decided to use it as his own desktop litter box, and now said Rolodex was in the garbage.

Two months running the center and Josie was only driving it deeper into financial ruin. Taking over her mother's business had been a huge mistake. Josie was a marriage counselor, not a sex therapist, and she didn't have her mother's vast experience in the subject, either. She also didn't know squat about running a business, but her mother had begged, and Josie had given in, as usual.

She'd been wanting to come back home to San Francisco anyway, and a year of counseling about-to-divorce couples had skewed her perspective enough to believe that leading seminars with titles such as "Fifty Ways to Drive Him Wild" might be fun.

Josie stared at her discussion notes and tried not to think about the fact that in a matter of minutes she would have to talk about multiple orgasms like an expert when she'd never even encountered the mythical phenomenon herself. The elderly attendees of the seminar about to start, "Reawakening the Goddess: Great Sex After Sixty," were going to eat her alive.

Noise from the busy street outside invaded the lobby as the front door opened, and Josie looked up from the registration counter to see Miriam MacAfee, a long-time attendee of the center's seminars, heading straight for her. She had that purposeful look in her eye that people always get when they're about to scrub the toilet or offer advice. She stopped on the other side of the registration counter and placed one liver-spotted hand on top of Josie's.

"Is your mother coming back soon, dear?"

"Hi, Mrs. MacAfee. I'm afraid not. She's planning to stay in Prague until next year."

"That's a shame. The center just isn't the same without her."

"Tell me about it."

"You're doing a fine job, though," she said, studying Josie closely.

"Thanks."

"You just seem a little uptight." She leaned forward and dropped her voice to a whisper. "Having a bit of a drought?"

"Excuse me?"

"Your sex life, honey. Is it all dried up?" She gave Josie's hand a reassuring squeeze.

Josie's face burned. Was Miriam MacAfee, seventy-year-old piano teacher, really asking her about her sex life? Could this get any more bizarre?

"Um. Well…"

"It's okay. I understand."

"You do?"

"Oh, sure. Your professional reputation hinges on your having a frisky sex life."

"It does?" Boy, was she ever in trouble.

"And it's embarrassing to a young girl like you to admit things aren't happening in bed. But let me tell you, once you get to be my age, you learn there's no shame in needing a good roll in the hay."

"Hmm." Josie set aside the phone book and made a show of studying her class roster.

Miriam leaned over the counter and peered at the class discussion notes Josie had set aside. "Looks like we'll be having quite a discussion tonight. Have you had any practical experience with multiple orgasms?"

"Um, well…"

"Oh, dear, you haven't, have you?"

"Actually, I'm very familiar with the subject," she lied.

Great, she might as well sew a scarlet L for loser on her chest, if near-strangers were able to look at her and see that it had been far too long since her last sexual encounter. Maybe if she formally announced her problem, some willing male would take pity on her and turn her into a well-sexed woman. She already possessed the intellectual knowledge of sex to talk like a woman of experience, but what she needed was the action to back it up.

And now she had no idea how she was going to conduct tonight's seminar wondering if the entire class could tell by looking at her that she desperately needed to get laid.

Desperately was the operative word. Josie felt her cheeks redden again just thinking about the outrageous dreams she'd been having ever since she'd started working at the center. All the sex talk was affecting her. Heaven help her if she passed a cute guy on the street. She'd spend the rest of the day fantasizing about him until she had herself worked up into a frenzy of monumental proportions.

Miriam finished nosing through the class discussion notes and gave Josie an apologetic grin. "I'm being quite the pest, aren't I?"

"Not at all."

"I just hate to see a young woman like you not having the time of her life, that's all." She patted Josie's hand and wandered over to a group of women chatting near the window.

Several more students filed in the front door and gathered in the reception area, talking and laughing. Josie counted gray and silver heads. Six, seven, eight, nine—that meant all attendees were present and she could begin the seminar anytime now. She took a deep breath and exhaled slowly. The idea of discussing sensual lubricants and unreliable erections with a group of grandmothers didn't exactly sit well with Josie, but here she was. Too late to back out now.

She'd left San Francisco precisely to avoid this kind of humiliation. In fact, the Lovers for Life Center was one of the main reasons Josie had fled the city after college. She'd wanted to establish a life of her own far away from her mother's scandalous reputation in the psychological community, and she'd hoped to distance herself from sex therapy.

So much for distance.

"Okay, ladies. If you'll find yourselves a seat in the class area, we can get started."

Every client present was a regular at the center, so they automatically headed for the comfortable circle of armchairs that made up the formal classroom. For more hands-on classes, or if the students just preferred it, a floor area with mats and pillows was also set up for seminars, but these women weren't interested in getting themselves to and from the floor.

Josie shuffled through her class notes, suddenly feeling panicked. They were going to eat her alive. Miriam MacAfee was right; she had no sex life. How could she speak knowledgeably about sex to women who'd already spent a lifetime building their knowledge and experience?

Her intellectual understanding of sex would have to be good enough. Her mother had started teaching her about the birds and the bees before most girls had even thought of putting Barbie and Ken dolls in scandalous positions. Josie understood the chemistry of sexual arousal the way some women understood how to throw together a perfect dinner or to match up a great outfit. She knew what made an unforgettable sexual experience.

Intellectually, anyway. But sex wasn't the kind of thing you could simply study in a book.

She glanced out the front picture window at a passing cable car and briefly contemplated escaping, running away to some place where no one had ever heard of the Lovers for Life Center or her mother, Rafaela Marcus. No time for fantasies though; she had nine frisky grandmas waiting to talk sex.

Josie went to the seminar area and took her seat in

the circle of chairs. The murmurs of conversation stopped and silence filled the room.

She cleared her throat, sat up straight in her chair, and began. "Sensual lubricants. Necessary evil, or the easy way in?"

THE SIGN IN THE WINDOW of the Lovers for Life Center read, Finding Your Inner Orgasm: Learn To Make Loud And Lusty Love A Reality In Your Life! Sign Up Now For Classes." Trent O'Reilly had seen quite a few weird topics advertised on that sign over the years, but this was definitely one of the most bizarre.

Only in San Francisco could a sex school exist without anyone batting an eye. Trent knew the owner, had even grown up with her daughter Josie, although *she* was another matter.

Dr. Rafaela Marcus was a local celebrity in her own right, and she'd turned her school for the sexually impaired into a San Francisco landmark. Trent had never liked the idea of giving directions to his own sporting goods store by saying it was right next door to a place called the Lovers for Life Center.

He peered in the window, hoping to catch a glimpse of Josie Marcus. No luck. The lobby was empty. A class was probably in session, but he had no idea when it would let out, and he wanted to catch Josie before she left the building. Trent had avoided an unpleasant task for too long. He couldn't put it off any longer.

But his feet remained frozen in place. He never had been able to resist Josie, and he couldn't help worrying that now would be no different. She was, after all, still the object of his erotic fantasies, still the girl he'd grown up chasing but never catching. What if nothing had changed?

No, that was just crazy thinking. *Everything* had changed since that night three years ago. That Ocean Beach fiasco had marked the last time he would ever be a fool for Josie again.

Trent glared across the sidewalk at his car, parked at the curb. Fueling his resolve to face up to Josie and to demand the back rent was the brand-new dent he'd spotted a few minutes ago on the formerly pristine pearl-white bumper of his Porsche.

A dent with traces of red paint. And a foot away sat the bumper of the offending vehicle. An all-too-familiar red Saab convertible with enough body damage to suggest the owner was a lousy driver, as he knew Josie was. She was especially lousy at parallel parking, he remembered from the time in high school when she'd parallel parked right up onto a curb and into the window of a Thai restaurant.

Trent entered the Lovers for Life Center and surveyed the reception area, a gathering of overstuffed purple-velvet chairs and love seats. The entire place was done up in pale birch wood and shades of purple, a color Rafaela must have determined was conducive to sex talk.

Beyond the reception area, there was a registration desk and a library area of books and videos to one side. Trent wandered over and glanced at the spines of the books, titles such as *Every Woman's Fantasy* and *The Language of Lovers* catching his eye. Just past the library he could see the main classroom, beyond which there was a smaller classroom and a door marked Office down the hallway toward the back of the building.

Trent perked his ears up to listen to the seminar in session. Okay, so maybe he shouldn't be eavesdropping on people's sex problems, but he'd always wondered about the details of what went on here.

"…and multiple orgasms are still certainly achievable."

Laughter from the class. Someone commented on her husband not being aware of such a thing. Then another woman spoke up to offer her experience on the subject.

Hey, Trent had experiences to offer on the subject, too. He imagined the reaction his popping into a class in session might elicit in Josie. Grinning, he headed for the classroom.

Just as he reached the doorway, Josie was saying, "How many of you here feel as if your partners have less sex drive than…" Her voice trailed off when she spotted him standing at the back of the room. Her face instantly lost its color. "…you do?"

Murmurs, several titters from the students, all of whom were female, sitting in a circle of chairs, and old enough to be his grandmother.

What the hell was going on? This wasn't the crowd he usually saw wandering into the center.

Trent was beginning to regret his decision to pop in on the class in session when he caught the look of pure panic on Josie's face.

The sight of her live and in person, only twenty feet away, made his stomach drop to his feet. It had been too long; it hadn't been long enough. She both repelled him and attracted him with some mysterious force he couldn't resist.

And damn if she still didn't turn him on.

She looked even better than before—and she'd been a knock-out back then. Her wavy blond hair was shorter now, falling to her shoulders in a professional-woman sort of style. It made her look grown up, and inexplicably the thought of Josie the Tease being a woman now got him hard. The curves beneath her black suit were more grown-up, too, soft-and-naked-in-bed grown-up.

He shouldn't be thinking such thoughts. This was how she always lured him in. But not again. He wasn't going to take that bait again.

"I—I'm sorry, no visitors allowed in this class," Josie said.

He considered slipping out gracefully, but a plump woman with frizzy white hair spoke up.

"Aw, come on, let the young stud stay. We could use a male perspective on this topic."

"Yeah, let him stay," someone else called out.

Trent flashed a weak grin. Talking sex with a roomful of grandmas was about as far as he could get from his idea of a good time. He was suddenly feeling like a bumbling schoolboy for reasons that had nothing to do with the presence of his childhood playmate or her maddening sex appeal.

But if staying meant driving Josie any crazier, he was all for it, and she looked as if she'd just swallowed a bowling ball. Perfect.

"Everyone in the group would have to agree to having a guest present." Josie paused, apparently waiting for a voice of protest. "Please raise your hand if you'd like him to stay."

All of the women raised their hands, and Josie shot Trent a menacing glare. "It looks like you can stay. Our topic is how women over the age of sixty can maintain an exciting sex life. I'm sure you'll be intrigued."

So maybe he didn't have much to offer on the subject, but he took an empty seat near the door anyway and settled in to watch Josie squirm. Collecting the rent was turning out to be a hell of a lot more interesting than he'd imagined.

"Okay, who can share solutions you've found to re-invigorate your partner's interest?" Josie asked, her voice almost imperceptibly shaky.

A woman to the left spoke up. "I once dressed myself up in nothing but the sports pages. Problem was, once he got the newspaper off of me, he sat down to read it and I fell asleep."

"I've found reading erotic literature out loud together can really heat things up," another woman offered.

Not a bad idea. Trent filed the tip in his memory.

A woman wearing blue rhinestone cat-eye glasses and a matching bejeweled shirt turned to him. "What does our guest suggest for catching a man's interest?"

Okay, maybe he'd gotten more than a little out of his league here. Trent grinned and shrugged. "I can't imagine you ladies having trouble seducing men."

One woman said, "Our trouble is, we need men that still have a pulse."

The rest of the group nodded in agreement.

"Yeah, like Cutie Pie over there," said another woman.

"What are you doing Saturday night, honey?" said a third.

Josie now looked as if the bowling ball was making its way through her digestive tract. "Ladies! We're getting off topic here. I'm afraid our guest is more of a distraction than anything, so—"

"Say no more. I'll wait outside," Trent interrupted, holding up his hands in defeat and thankful for the easy out.

Several of the seminar attendees groaned their disappointment, and the woman next to Trent blew him a kiss as he vacated his chair.

Out in the lobby again, he sunk onto one of the leather sofas, prepared to wait as long as necessary to corner Josie. He grabbed the nearest magazine on the table next to him and checked out the cover. *The Secret Garden: Erotic Stories for Women.* Hmm, interesting.

He was halfway through the story of Sabine and her nubile young lover when women began to file out of the class area. Glancing around for Josie, he spotted her at the registration desk talking to a student.

When she looked up at him, he could have sworn he saw raw desire flash in her eyes. But that must have been a mistake. The Josie he knew never gazed hungrily at men. She made the men do all the gazing and hungering.

He started to put down the erotica magazine, but then thought the better of it and rolled it up to stick in his back pocket for later—purely for research into the female psyche. With Josie still watching him, he approached the desk.

Two gray-haired women passed him and he heard one of them whisper, "Oh, honey, if I were twenty years younger, I'd have my way with that one."

He glanced around to see their gazes fixed on his Levi's—or rather, what the jeans concealed. Trent's neck burned and, turning back to Josie, he saw from her wry grin that she had overheard the comment, too.

"Don't let it go to your head. They're just all riled up from the seminar."

"Right."

They were so close he could reach out and touch her now if he wanted to—the closest they'd been in years. All his senses became hyperaware of Josie. Her perfume was something fruity and intoxicating, and the smooth curve of her jaw begged for his touch. But, as he'd learned the hard way, touching Josie always led to trouble.

"And don't ever drop in on one of my classes again."

"Sorry, I didn't think you'd mind." His grin betrayed the fact that he'd known very well it would drive her crazy.

"Finally come to welcome me back to the city?" she asked, as if she didn't know she was two months late on the center's rent payments. Or that she had used the Braille method of parallel parking today behind his car.

"No, I came to offer you a free parking lesson."

"What's that supposed to mean?"

"It means that since you hit my car, I can't ignore your presence any longer."

Now there was a lie. He couldn't have ignored her presence if his Porsche depended on it. Ever since she'd arrived back in town, he'd been unwillingly focused on her comings and goings.

Even as he'd listed in his head all the reasons he didn't want to see Josie, all the reasons he was over her for good, he constantly watched for her to pass by his store window.

Trent took note that there was now a stiffness in her posture, a strain around her eyes, which was new since the last time he'd been this close to her. She looked like a woman who needed…a good roll in the hay. If he were letting his urges influence his decision-making, he'd say he was just the man for the job.

"I didn't hit your car, I just nudged it a little."

"You nudged a thousand-dollar dent into the bumper."

Her jaw sagged and her eyes registered horror.

Trent instantly regretted making up an estimate. "Maybe not a thousand, but Porsche body work isn't exactly cheap. I hope you've got insurance coverage."

She frowned. "Just liability, and I may have let it lapse this month. Are you sure I put the dent there?"

"Positive."

Josie slumped back against the counter and expelled a ragged breath. "It's one thing after another. I'm sorry about your car."

He stared at her, his arms crossed. If she was trying to guilt him into calling them even, he wouldn't fall for it.

"Give me a bill from the repair shop, and I'll pay you when I can."

"Which will be when? Right after you pay me for the past two months' rent on the center?"

She winced. "Oh, that. I was hoping you hadn't noticed."

"Believe me, I notice when someone owes me six grand." It was an obscene amount for two months' rent, but normal for San Francisco these days.

"My mother left the finances in a shambles."

"Rafaela was never late with the rent."

"She took all the excess money in the business account when she left for Prague."

"Why would she do that?"

Josie shrugged. "To finance her boyfriend's literary efforts."

Rafaela, Trent knew from her harmless flirting, had a thing for younger men and, judging by the tone of her voice, her daughter obviously didn't approve. Not that he could blame Josie. As much as he'd teased her when they were kids, he could imagine how hard it was to be

Rafaela's daughter, to have a mother so wild that the only option was to become a stick in the mud.

But for a stick in the mud, Josie sure had a strange effect on him. Something about her too-wide mouth never failed to illicit pornographic thoughts, and those small, round breasts of hers... On any other woman he never would have given them a second glance, but on Josie's compact frame, he couldn't help but imagine how they'd feel in his palms, in his mouth.

He forced the unwelcome thoughts out of his head.

"Kind of funny that you went into counseling at all, considering how you always tried so hard not to be like your mother. Why marriage counseling?"

"I guess because I came from a broken home, I wanted to help other people avoid it."

"Makes sense." Never mind that she was sort of a head case herself. She'd been such a cock tease in high school, she'd probably caused countless horny teenage boys to seek counseling.

Josie smiled and waved goodbye to one of the last grandmas to leave the lobby.

"So what brought you back to the city? Did you get tired of breaking up marriages?"

Her smile vanished and her eyes narrowed at him, but she resisted taking his bait.

"My mother needed someone to run the place, and I needed the job. Simple as that."

"Life in the Midwest wasn't all it was cracked up to be?"

"I was living in Boston, not the Midwest."

"Same difference. Did you get fired or something?"

"No, I just wanted to move back to San Francisco."

"I'm flattered," he joked. "I've never had a woman move cross-country to be near me."

"You're as deluded as ever," she said casually, but her stiff posture told volumes. Regardless of her words, she obviously wasn't comfortable talking about their attraction to each other.

That fact intrigued him far more than he would have liked. *Focus on the task at hand, man.* "You still haven't told me how you plan to come up with your late rent payments."

She squeezed her eyes shut tight, probably doing mental calculations of what it would cost to run off to Mexico instead of paying him.

"I can maybe give you one month's rent in another three or four weeks."

"That's not good enough." Trent felt a pang of guilt, then reminded himself that this was Josie he was talking to.

He had every right to bring a little discomfort into her life after what she'd put him through. Still, he was a sucker for a damsel in distress. And she looked like one seriously distressed damsel right now.

"What do you want? A pound of flesh?"

"Not a bad idea. Maybe we can work out a deal."

"What kind of deal?"

What kind of deal, indeed?

On the counter lay a stack of lavender flyers announcing upcoming seminars. He picked one up and scanned it out of curiosity. "The Art of Sensual Touch. The Role of the Five Senses in Arousal… Dangerous Places: Sexual Excitement Outside The Bedroom." The list went on.

Josie shifted her weight forward and he caught the scent of her perfume again. He suddenly imagined that scent on her naked skin, intensifying with the sweat of

their lovemaking in some dangerous place, some trop-
ical snake-filled forest.

Everything about her had always made him think of
sex. Even the nerdy little glasses she was wearing. He
didn't care much for women in glasses, and he didn't
go for intellectual snobs like Josie, so it frustrated the
hell out of him that every time she was around he turned
into a horny teenager again.

And these seminar subjects weren't doing a thing to
quell his libido.

An idea was forming in Trent's head. Something slippery that he was almost afraid to grasp hold of. Something involving Josie, and him, and an old score to settle. Something involving revenge.

"What's this 'Art of Sensual Touch'?" he asked.

Josie sucked her lower lip between her teeth and it
emerged full and wet. Trent watched, mesmerized, not
sure what was more interesting, her mouth or the im-
pending course description. "It's one of our more popular seminars."

"Care to explain?"

"You can use your imagination, right?"

Oh, yeah, his imagination was working overtime. "Is
this a hands-on class?"

She sighed. "Parts of it, yes."

Hmm. The idea was fully formed in his head now,
just sitting there, offering him a chance to accomplish
what he never would have thought possible—to get San
Francisco's biggest tease, Josie Marcus, into bed; to
give her a taste of her own medicine; to finally even the
score between them.

"Could I speak to you privately in your office?"

Josie wrinkled her nose, already smelling something

fishy. But he had to convince her otherwise, that what he was about to say was absolutely true.

"I guess." She motioned for him to follow.

He trailed her down the hallway, making a great effort not to watch her firm rear end as she walked. They passed the classroom to the last door, where she flicked on a light to reveal an office that was pure Rafaela Marcus. Butter-soft purple leather sofa and chairs, lots of funky art pieces decorating the walls and shelves, a wide birch desk stacked with books and papers. He wondered if Josie felt at home here or if she was just trying on her mother's life for size.

"Have a seat." She motioned him to the sofa as she sat in a nearby chair. When he sat, she asked, "So what's the big secret?"

Trent made like a man about to admit something supremely embarrassing. He glanced at his feet, ran his hand through his hair a few times, cleared his throat.

"So you're pretty much an expert on sex, right?" he asked.

"I prefer to think of myself as an expert on romantic relationships."

"Which means sex."

She blinked. "Sex is one small component of romance."

"Sounds like you know more about it than I do then." He cleared his throat. "I need your help."

Her eyes widened. "With sex?"

Trent wore what he hoped was his most earnest expression. "I'm having some problems. In the bedroom. My girlfriends seem to be leaving unsatisfied."

Josie's jaw sagged and it took all his willpower not to laugh. She glanced at his crotch and said, "I don't know what to say."

"Say you'll give me private lessons, one on one, just the two of us. Help me figure out what I'm doing wrong in the bedroom and fix it."

A little strangled sound escaped her throat. She covered her mouth with one hand and produced a fake cough, then another, and another.

It was time to make his offer clear. "You give me two months of sex lessons, and I'll call us even on the back rent payments."

2

JOSIE HEARD HERSELF sputtering, then snapped her mouth shut until she could think clearly enough to form words. Could Trent O'Reilly, the most wanted stud in their high school graduating class, really be sitting in front of her asking her to teach him how to please a woman?

She looked up into his blue eyes, which always held a spark of mischief, only to find him gazing back at her completely earnest. His trademark smirk was gone, too. Trent, with his raven hair cut stylishly short and his outdoorsman tan, his five o'clock shadow and his lean athlete's body, sat in front of Josie reminding her of her every teenage fantasy—most of her adult ones, too. But she'd never imagined him asking for *this*.

Josie had learned in her work that anything was possible. And it was true that some attractive men tended not to work very hard in the bedroom, figuring it was enough for a woman just to *be* in bed with the likes of them. Maybe Trent was an honest enough guy to admit the error of his ways, but still…

"I can't give you private sex lessons!" she screeched when she'd found the power to speak again.

"Sure you can. Do a bang-up job and I won't even make you pay for the dent on my car."

"You want *sex* lessons. As in, *me* having sex with *you?*"

Just spelling out his request was enough to make her dizzy with desire. And the fact that Trent had only grown more gorgeous in the past three years didn't help matters. The anxiety of her predicament battled with a warm fuzzy feeling between her legs to influence her decision-making abilities.

"I doubt I could learn much just sitting across the room from you."

"I don't think that's a good idea. I mean, considering our history—"

The image of Trent in her rearview mirror at Ocean Beach three years ago flashed into Josie's mind. She'd just tossed his shirt and pants out the car window for him; his face registering only disbelief, not anger, as she'd driven off.

"It's the perfect solution," he said.

"There is the matter of the bad feelings between us. Do you really think you'd get anything out of these… these…lessons? From me?"

"Oh, yeah. I'll get quite a bit out of them."

"I'm sorry, but I can't help you with your problem. You'll have to think of some other way for me to repay you."

"You're sure about that?"

"Positive."

Trent shook his head and stood up. "I'm sorry we couldn't work out a deal. I'll expect your full two months back rent payment on Monday."

Panic seized Josie's chest. "I've already told you I can't pay that soon."

"Have you read the terms of your lease?"

"No," she lied.

"The lease says I have the right to evict you if one month's rent goes thirty days past due."

"But…" But what? She owed him thousands of dollars and she didn't have a clue how she was going to pay up.

"Have a nice day, Josie."

She watched him exit the office, realizing exactly how in need of sex she was when the sight of his firm jeans-clad rear end temporarily erased her worries.

Josie sat at the desk in a daze, afraid to leave the office until she was absolutely sure Trent had left the building. How had her life come to this? A few short months ago she'd been living a perfectly normal existence in Boston. She'd had a secure job as a marriage counselor, and it had been the future she'd always envisioned for herself.

Well, sort of.

She hadn't envisioned marriage counseling being such depressing work, and she hadn't ever imagined herself staying home on the weekends redecorating her tiny apartment—that no one ever saw—over and over again. She hadn't pictured herself having such a dismal personal life, with no boyfriend, no late-night lover, not even an annoying ex to call to beg her for a second chance every now and then.

The friends she'd made in Boston were all married or seriously dating, and they'd all considered it their personal duty to find Josie a boyfriend. The problem was that they were all a little too good at it, tracking down every eligible hunk in the city of Boston. Josie couldn't admit to her friends that she simply wasn't capable of having an intimate relationship with a sexually attractive man; that every time she got close to going all the way with a man who turned her on, she became paralyzed with fear that she'd lose control and end up like her mother, a woman ruled by her passion for men.

When Josie turned down one date after another, her friends got annoyed. Over time they'd invited her to fewer and fewer get-togethers until finally she'd rarely heard from anyone.

Growing up with a male-bimbo-chasing mother like Rafaela Marcus had taught Josie the dangers of physical attraction, and working as a marriage counselor had exposed her to the darker side of romance. She wasn't ready for any kind of committed relationship.

But maybe what she did need was a lover. Someone to ease the burning ache inside her a few times a week. Or more.

Here she was, back in her hometown, still pitifully alone, with the last guy she wanted to see suddenly making her the most outrageous proposition she'd ever heard. Was this the universe's idea of a joke? Was Trent O'Reilly—the boy who'd chased her with snails in kindergarten, the kid who'd pulled up her skirt at the bus stop in the eighth grade, the guy who'd taken her to the prom in high school only because his first three choices had already had dates—really her only option right now?

A few years ago his offer might not have been so complicated. But now… She'd pretty much ruined any chance they'd had of having a simple relationship when she'd chickened out at Ocean Beach. Trent would never let her live down his being ditched just when he thought they were going to get it on.

The problem with Trent was, he was too tempting. The sexual attraction between them was too strong, too volatile, too easy to lose control of. Josie knew because they'd come so close more than once before. On prom night, and again during their misguided encounter three years ago. When things heated up between Trent and Josie, the temperature turned scorching, and Josie ran from the heat.

She could still recall every important detail of that night—the way Trent's skin had tasted faintly of salt from the unexpected summer heat wave, the way he'd moved so slowly, teasing her and tempting her until she was almost out of her mind with wanting him, the expression of confusion he'd worn when she'd asked him to get out of the car.

Never mind that he'd been naked. No one was around. He'd simply shrugged and climbed out her passenger door, probably assuming she had an embarrassing birth control procedure to attend to. Or perhaps a sex-in-the-sand fantasy to act out.

Most of all, she'd never forget the terror that had seized her at having come so close to having sex with Trent. So very close to a fantasy she couldn't dream of living up to. That terror had struck her a handful of times, always with men she truly desired.

It was her most embarrassing secret, that she could only make love to men who didn't excite her. In all her twenty-nine years she'd only had a few lovers, and she'd been forced to choose them for their lack of effect on her libido.

She rested her head on her arms on top of the desk, but that put her face-to-face with the desk calendar, and that made her start counting months. She counted back eleven months, twelve months, thirteen months…and then her head snapped back up. She sat bolt upright, her mind reeling at the realization that it had been a *long* time since she'd last had sex.

Miriam MacAfee was right; she'd been able to just

look at Josie and tell. Maybe there was some tenseness in her shoulders, a desperate look in her eyes, a stiffness in her walk. Whatever it was, she needed to get rid of it. Fast. Aside from the fact that she missed having sex, there was also the matter of her not being able to credibly give sensuality seminars if she could remember nothing about the subject herself.

She found her purse on the floor near the desk and dug out her small three-year personal calendar, the place she recorded all the major and minor events in her life. She flipped back through the months, searching for some proof that her count was wrong.

A knock on the office door halted her and she prayed it wasn't Trent again. Before she could ask who was there, Erika Li, the center's receptionist and all-around handygirl, poked her head in.

"You busy?"

"Not exactly. Come on in."

Erika flopped down into the chair opposite Josie's desk, her gauzy red Gypsy-style dress billowing around her and then settling. "I need a break from the horny people."

"You've come to the wrong place, then."

Her eyebrows perked up. "You? Sexually needy?"

"Why is that surprising?"

"I just figured the daughter of Rafaela Marcus would have her sex life all worked out, you know?"

"I'd first need to get a sex life before I could have it all worked out."

Josie turned her attention back to her personal calendar and flipped through the months again. Back further and further, until she finally came to a September, nearly two years back, during which her love life had still been alive and kicking.

"It's been almost two years since I've had sex."

"You mean two *months*, right?" Erika asked, dead serious.

"No, two years. I just double-checked my calendar."

"Are you sure you didn't count wrong? Let me see that thing." Erika snatched the calendar and flipped back through the months.

"The big events are marked with an asterisk in the left-hand corner."

"Maybe you just forgot to record some of the less memorable encounters?"

"Impossible."

Erika shook her head when her count of the asterisk-free months yielded the same sad truth as Josie's. "You need to get laid."

"I don't even have any prospects. Electrical appliances are starting to look sexy."

"Oh, you have prospects. I bet you're just too cautious."

"You sound like my mother."

"She's a wise woman."

"My mother's a deviant and you know it."

Erika smiled. "Let me guess, you go so far out of your way not to be like her, you've turned yourself into a nun."

Ouch. That felt a little too close to being the truth. Josie shifted uncomfortably in her chair.

"It's this center. How am I supposed to keep it alive while the woman born to run it is playing house with her Bohemian stud boy in Prague?"

"Your mom and her boys... What ever happened to your father, anyway? Were they married?"

Josie had barely known her father, and Rafaela had never been much interested in talking about him. "All

I know is that they were married, but he left when I was a baby. Couldn't take the responsibility or something like that.''

Erika narrowed her eyes as if reading the future on Josie's forehead. "I bet you're afraid enjoying sex will turn you into your mother."

Blushing, Josie looked away. Again, Erika's comment fell dangerously close to the truth. "Your degree's in massage therapy, not sex therapy."

She shrugged. "I've worked here long enough to pick up a few pointers."

Josie glared at her calendar. How could she let the months—the years!—slip by like that? She was supposed to be in the prime of her life, not withering away like her maiden aunt Mitsy.

"I'm not afraid of sex, I just have bad luck."

Erika leaned forward and planted her palms on the desk. "Does this sex crisis have anything to do with the hottie next door who just slipped out of your office a few minutes ago?"

"Trent O'Reilly has nothing to do with my dry spell." And that was true, wasn't it? He couldn't possibly have influenced her comatose sex life. Josie's stomach flip-flopped as the truth began to creep up on her.

"But I bet he could help you end it." The gold stud in Erika's pierced tongue glittered as she caught it between her teeth and wiggled it.

Josie's face burned. She couldn't tell anyone about Trent's offer, even if she had refused. It was just too embarrassing to think that the center's financial problems had come down to her trading sex lessons for rent. Sex lessons, for heaven's sake!

But some little niggling thought was bugging Josie. If she needed sex, and Trent needed lessons...

Erika leaned in close. "What did he want, anyway?"

"The rent. We're two months late."

"Ooh, I can think of a trade he might like."

If only she knew how right she was. Josie cleared her throat and shifted in her chair. "Don't even go there."

She felt her friend's speculative gaze. "Don't look so bummed. You're supposed to be happy when you become indebted to a calendar-worthy hunk. Allows more time to figure out how to get him into bed."

"Indebted is the last thing I need to be right now."

"In fact, it wouldn't be an inappropriate response to update your panty drawer now, buy a few new push-up bras—"

"Erika..."

"For Rafaela's daughter, you sure are a prude."

"I'm not a prude, I'm just normal. You've developed a warped sense of sexual norms working here."

"It's just the opposite. I see what people are really like in this job, and you, my friend, are sexually repressed."

"I am not."

"When was the last time you had really hot sex? I'm guessing more than two years ago, since that last time wasn't even good enough to call for a repeat performance."

Josie studied a chipped fingernail. "Depends on how you define 'really hot sex.' I've had sexual relationships." With a few guys, none of them very memorable, but at least she'd stayed awake. That counted for something, didn't it?

Erika gave her a pitying look. "Mind-blowing, bed-rocking, toe-curling, go-all-night sex. Please tell me you've had it at least once."

All night? She couldn't recall any of her boyfriends ever having needed more than twenty minutes, thirty tops.

"Do yourself a favor and go find someone to give you a screaming orgasm."

Josie tried not to laugh. "Does it have to be a screaming one?"

"You won't regret it if you do, but someday when you're old and your arthritis keeps you from getting into all the more creative positions, you *will* regret it if you don't."

"Arthritis wasn't slowing down any of my students today," she joked. But maybe Erika was right. Maybe she was a prude. Maybe she'd spent so many years trying to be different from her mother that she'd taken it to the extreme.

One of her more embarrassing high school memories flashed into her mind—hosting a sleep-over with three of her friends. Josie had felt like dying when Rafaela had proceeded to hold an impromptu sex-ed class for the teenage girls. That was the night Josie had vowed she was going to be the exact opposite of her sex-obsessed mother.

Maybe she'd taken that vow a little too far.

"Trent O'Reilly is the stuff wild sexual flings are made of. He's the perfect candidate for an unforgettable affair."

Sex with *Trent?* Could she do it? Could she really spend not just one night, but two months, getting intimate with the guy she'd spent most of her lifetime running away from? Could she really teach him how to be the perfect lover?

"Do you know about our history?"

"Rafaela told me you guys were childhood sweethearts or something."

"Or something. Definitely not sweethearts. We grew up together in the Richmond District, and there have been a few, uh, encounters."

"But no sex?"

"Just a couple of close calls. Last time was three years ago, when I was still in college. We ended up in my car together, going for a ride to the beach. Things heated up, then I freaked out and drove off with his underwear."

Erika looked perplexed. "Where was he when you drove away?"

"I kicked him out of the car and left him on the beach. It wasn't exactly my finest hour."

"Why'd you keep his underwear?"

"They were on the floor—I didn't see them."

"Boxers or briefs? I'm guessing boxers."

"Mmm-hmm." Josie nodded. She kept to herself the fact that she still had Trent's boxers hidden in the glove compartment of her Saab.

"I swear, you therapists are always the most screwed-up people around."

Josie started to protest but thought better of it. Maybe Erika wasn't so far off base on that charge.

"Just admit you'd like to do the wild thing with Trent."

"Me and the rest of the heterosexual females in San Francisco."

"So you admit it!"

"It's purely sexual. Personality-wise, I can't stand the guy. But physically, yes, I can think of a few ways to entertain myself with him."

"There you have it then, someone to end your drought." Erika stood and headed for the door, her red dress swishing as she walked.

Josie didn't bother to argue, and then she realized it was because she didn't *want* to argue the point. Somehow, without her brain's approval, her libido had already decided Trent was the solution to her problem.

For the next two months, anyway.

TRENT LEANED AGAINST the counter of Extreme Sports and surveyed the store. A full-time salesclerk, Max, was talking to a young couple in the bike section about their options for mountain bikes, and two regulars in the store were browsing the summer athletic wear. Trent didn't have the energy to do anything more than remain propped behind the counter, thanks to a lousy night's sleep.

Thanks to his meeting with Josie yesterday.

Okay, so it was his own fault for trying to entangle himself with her again, but now that he had, he couldn't stop replaying their encounter in his head. He couldn't stop thinking about all the ways he could have teased and tempted her if she'd accepted his offer. All night long, he'd thought about it.

Damn, Josie drove him crazy. No one should be able to have so much control over him. Just having her right next door every day was enough to make him think seriously about running for the hills, following through on his occasional dream of selling Extreme Sports and moving to Tahoe. He could lead adventure tours full-time and never have to deal with that woman again.

Trent pushed himself up from the counter and vowed

to find some busywork, anything to take his mind off of…the woman walking in the front door.

He leveled his gaze at Josie as she made her way through the store, a leather notebook tucked under one arm, her expression carefully blank. She wore a suit again, this one navy-blue and cut to hint at her curves, but her hair was slightly mussed, and he could see, as she came closer, dark circles under her eyes. Perhaps he hadn't been the only one watching the minutes tick by last night.

"Morning, Josie."

"I need to speak with you in private, if you can spare the time."

Trent maintained a poker face. "Hey, Max, I'll be in the back for a while."

Max looked up and nodded, while Trent told himself not to get too hopeful about Josie's presence. She'd probably been up all night working up a payment plan—and not the sexual one he hoped for, either.

He led her down a hallway cluttered with boxes and sports equipment, then through the door to his small office.

"Have a seat." He motioned to a giant baseball-glove-shaped chair, restraining a smile as Josie hesitated for a moment before perching herself on its edge.

Trent pulled out his desk chair and turned it around to straddle it, then realized his mistake when he took in his prime view of Josie's legs. His position pulled his jeans tight and left no room for certain changes that were bound to take place if he kept staring up her skirt.

She cleared her throat, opened her leather notebook and removed a piece of paper. That was when he noticed her shaking hand.

"I've given your offer a great deal of thought…."

Oh, yeah?

"And I've come to the conclusion that it could be a mutually beneficial arrangement if we both approached it in a serious and professional manner."

"So, you want to have serious and professional sex lessons?"

"I—I would like our relationship to be a professional one, but for the sake of the lessons, I'm sure we'll need to assume whatever mood is appropriate for the occasion."

"You've got a way of making even the tawdriest scenario sound boring, you know."

Her nostrils flared, the only sign that she didn't appreciate his observation.

"Sorry, I'll shut up now," he said, forcing a serious countenance. This was almost too good to be true.

"I have some stipulations for you before I can agree to anything."

"Okay, shoot."

"As your instructor, I feel it's important that I guide and control the lessons at all times." Her voice wavered.

"Sounds reasonable."

"I choose the subject matter based on what I determine to be the areas in which you need improvement."

His first instinct was to protest, but Trent bit his tongue and waited. He wanted to hear what else she had to say.

"And I'll need you to complete this questionnaire, so I'll have a clear idea of your current knowledge base." She held out the piece of paper, and Trent took it, intrigued.

He scanned the list of multiple-choice and short-answer questions. *What is your sexual orientation? How many lovers have you had? What percentage would you say have left unsatisfied? Describe your ideal lover. List the five most important qualities you believe you should possess as a lover. Describe your favorite sexual fantasy.*

Whoa.

He looked up at Josie, who was watching him, her expression completely serious.

"This is kind of personal, don't you think?"

"You did ask me for sex lessons. I can't think of a more personal subject matter than that. If I'm going to offer the lessons, I need to know you intimately."

"Babe, you will know me intimately by the time these lessons are done."

"This is the kind of information I'll need ahead of time, if you want the instruction tailored to your needs."

What the hell. He scanned the questions one more time and decided this could get interesting, considering how ill at ease Josie already seemed to be.

"Okay, let's go through the questions right now."

Her cheeks turned scarlet. "No, no, that's not necessary. I'll just leave the questionnaire with you and—"

"This way, if you need any explanation of my answers, you can just ask. Let's start with the first question. Answer A, strictly heterosexual. Question Two. 'How many lovers have you had?'"

He looked up to see that curiosity had won out over discomfort. Josie was listening, enthralled.

"A gentleman never tells. And besides, I don't keep count." He grinned at her, and she forced a smile back.

"I've never met a man who didn't know that number immediately."

"And I've never met a woman who was satisfied with the answer."

"It goes both ways," she said. "Most men like to believe they're going where no man has gone before."

This new boldness intrigued Trent. He wondered how far he could entice her to go. "You know, it's not really fair that I have to answer all these questions, when I don't know any of this information about you."

"I'm not the one who needs lessons."

"But how can I practice establishing intimacy with you when it's all one-sided? I think I'd be much more comfortable if this felt like a real relationship."

Her jaw sagged ever so slightly. She definitely hadn't anticipated this curve ball.

"If I know these things about you, it'll make it easier for me to please you," Trent offered.

"But—"

"We'll start with the easy questions. Sexual orientation?"

Josie licked her lips. He saw that boldness in her eyes again, and then he knew he had her. "Hetero."

"Number of sexual partners?"

"Less than five."

"But more than zero, right? You're supposed to be the expert here."

"More than zero, yes. And let me point out to you that number of sexual partners does not necessarily correlate with sexual expertise."

He watched her defend herself and his body responded with a surge of heat to his groin. He should have already been one of those lovers, and why hadn't he been? Why had she run away from him but not the others?

"Your turn." She grabbed the questionnaire from his

hand and read it. "'What percentage of your lovers have left unsatisfied?'"

Trent shrugged and made up a number. "Lately, I'd say eighty percent."

"Define 'lately.'"

"Since I've been mature enough to tell the difference between a woman who's faking and one who's really satisfied."

"I need a number."

He made like a man ashamed to admit the truth. "Five years."

Her brown eyes formed big Os. "And you're just now asking for help?"

"The opportunity just now presented itself. How about you?" he asked. "How many men have you left unsatisfied?"

Trent pinned Josie with his gaze, and her eyes sparked fire. He'd trapped her right where she didn't want to be, forced to admit she was a cock tease.

"Men I've gone to bed with? None."

"You know that's not a fair answer. Women leave men unsatisfied by *not* going to bed with them."

"You want me to count the number of men I haven't gone to bed with?" she said with a little smile, obviously enjoying the game again.

"Just the ones you left hot and bothered. But I realize that'll be a long list to compile, so we can move on to the next question for now, and you can give me your answer at our next meeting."

Josie narrowed her eyes at him, probably formulating a snappy comeback, but then she looked down at the questionnaire and smiled. "'Describe your favorite sexual fantasy.'"

He snatched the questionnaire back. "That's not the next question on the list."

She shrugged. "It's the next one I want to hear the answer to."

How could he tell her that his favorite sexual fantasies all involved her? Getting her so hot she couldn't take another moment of anticipation. Making love to her again and again, until they were both so sated they could only lie in a naked heap, resting up for the next round. Okay, so that was his adolescent fantasy. His adult ones were a bit more sophisticated. And detailed.

"Well, let's see… Do you want the R-rated version or the X-rated one?"

He was pretty sure her breathing quickened at that moment. She crossed and uncrossed her legs. "I suppose for the sake of accuracy, the X-rated version would be preferable."

"You're not gonna psychoanalyze me with this, are you?"

Josie shook her head. "This is purely for the sake of our lessons."

Trent leaned back, his chair resting against the wall and closed his eyes, picturing a favorite scenario he'd always wanted to act out with Josie. "I'm with a woman out in the woods somewhere. There's a shallow creek, and we're in it, playing around, splashing and stuff."

"Is she a woman you know well, or a stranger?"

"Someone I've known for a long time."

"Have you had sex with her before?"

"Maybe, maybe not. Doesn't matter."

"What happens after you've been playing in the water for a while?"

"We wrestle around, kiss, start taking each other's clothes off. Pretty soon we're naked."

He glanced at Josie's chest and an image of her, lit by moonlight in the car at Ocean Beach, came to him.

Her breasts were full and spilling over the top of a frilly white lace bra. He'd barely gotten to touch her before she'd kicked him out of the car and driven off.

"What happens next?" she asked.

"She drops to her knees there in the creek and starts to give me head, really slow and seductive, driving me crazy. Then she stops, moves her mouth up my body, kissing and licking."

He opened his eyes and caught Josie watching him like a starved animal.

"Do you kiss her back?"

"I rub my hands on her breasts, kiss and suck them. I kiss her, but she's in control. She stops me, gives me a wicked smile, and starts the splashing again."

"Do you splash back?"

"I try to pull her to me, but she catches me off balance and sends me sprawling back in the water. Then she takes off running, and I get up and chase her."

"What happens when you catch her?" Josie asked, almost breathless.

Trent leaned his head back and closed his eyes again, picturing the scene that had played out in his head too many times to count. There were many variations of it, but one constant: Josie, naked, wet and willing.

"We fall down together in the creek. The water's barely cool since it's midsummer and steaming hot outside. Her hands are all over me. I can tell she wants me now. She's really hot and bothered."

"How can you tell?"

Trent opened his eyes and let his gaze travel over her. "The way she's breathing, quick and shallow. The way she looks at me like I'm the last man on earth. The way her whole body seems tensed up, waiting for something."

"And what happens next?" she was bold enough to

ask, either ignoring or unaware that he'd just described her current state.

"I don't give in. We're having too much fun, and I want her to struggle for it."

"'It' as in sex?"

"Yeah. I make like I'm trying to escape, and she gets this wicked grin on her face. She tells me to be a good boy, and she pulls me over to a tree on the shore. She takes a vine and ties me to the tree."

"Are you sitting or standing?"

"Sitting on the ground, with my arms tied above my head. She climbs on my lap and rubs herself against my erection, then slides it inside of her. She's so wet and ready, it's all I can do to keep from coming right then."

"Why do you hold back?"

She'd just put on her psychology cap, trying to measure what he did and didn't know about pleasing a woman. It occurred to Trent that he could have made up a fantasy, something that illustrated his fictional ineptitude in the bedroom, but it was too late for that.

Besides, he was achieving his goal. Josie was clearly aroused by his fantasy, so now he knew he could turn her on. Pretty easily, too, it seemed.

"I want us to come at the same time. She starts riding me, slowly at first, then faster. I lick and suck her breasts, and she arches her back, moans. I can feel her getting wetter. She feels like a hot, ripe peach. I'm going insane. Her muscles start to contract around me, and then we climax in unison."

Beads of sweat had formed on Josie's upper lip, even though it was air-conditioner cool in his office. She pushed a strand of her hair behind one ear.

"You have a healthy imagination," she said, staring intently at the questionnaire.

"It's your turn. I want to hear your favorite sexual fantasy now."

Josie slapped her black notebook shut and rose from the giant baseball glove. "I just remembered—I need to go. I've got a seminar starting in ten minutes."

"No fair." Trent stood, too, and followed her as she edged her way toward the door. "I showed you mine, now you—"

"Please fill out the rest of the questionnaire and give it to me at our first lesson."

"Only if you fill one out, too."

She hesitated. "Okay, I will. When would you like to begin your lessons?"

"The sooner, the better. Are you free tonight?"

"T-tonight?" She exhaled slowly, then licked her lips. "Yes, I'm definitely free tonight. How about seven o'clock?"

"Seven is fine." Trent wrote down his address and handed it to Josie. "We'll meet at my place then."

She turned and looked at him when she reached the office door. "Interesting setting you chose for your fantasy."

"Hey, you said you wouldn't psychoanalyze."

A secretive smile spread across her lips. "Sorry, I couldn't resist. By the way, this woman in your fantasy, is she always the same person?"

"Why? Does it matter?"

"You've definitely got issues with her." Josie watched for his reaction, then turned and walked out the door.

Issues? Yeah, he had issues. If she only knew.

3

TONIGHT would be the test. If she could spend an evening with Trent without her panties melting, she could survive the next two months. Easy.

Yeah, right.

Josie glared up at the stoplight ahead and tried to ignore the man making rude hand gestures at her from the dump truck on the left. Apparently she'd made him angry, though she wasn't quite sure how. Something having to do with merging into his lane a few blocks back when she'd been a little distracted recalling Trent's fantasy.

Josie broke into a sweat just thinking about it again. She couldn't help picturing herself in the creek with him every time she remembered his words.

The images had been a little rough, the language coarser than she would have preferred, but he was a guy, after all.

She'd never witnessed a man say something so intimate outside of a counseling session, and it was a good thing, too, because she'd gotten so turned on she'd been useless the rest of the day at work.

The light turned green and Josie accelerated as fast as her decrepit car would allow. She flashed the dump truck guy a victorious look as she pulled ahead of him in traffic.

Josie wanted to end her sexual drought, but the

thought of ending it with Trent brought back that old shakiness, the fear she always ran away from. Okay, so she was a counselor, and she knew facing her fear would be the best way to conquer it. Probably the most fun way, too, in this case.

But how could she keep herself from freezing? How could she finally have sex with Trent after so many years of *not* having sex with him? And when she did give in to her urges, how could she possibly maintain any sense of professionalism or control?

She had to figure out some way to keep her sexual urges under control, so that *she* could remain in control. Trent was playing a game with her, she suspected, and she didn't know yet what the game was, only that she had an agenda of her own to pursue.

What she needed was a first lesson for him that would get the ball rolling fast. Once she'd let off nearly two years of sexual steam, she could relax and not worry so much about all her problems.

For now, though, what she needed was a shower. July in San Francisco usually meant seventy-degree temperatures, but today the thermometer had shot up to ninety, and suddenly the city that didn't need air-conditioning was a sweltering urban jungle. She'd driven home with the top down on her convertible to compensate for being hot all day at the center.

She arrived at home to find that she'd forgotten to open the windows that morning, and the inside of her apartment had turned into an oven. She hurried through the place opening windows, then headed straight for the bathroom, where she stripped off her work clothes and set the shower on lukewarm.

Perhaps a cold shower would have been more appropriate, but Josie was determined that tonight would not be a night for cold showers. She'd have her way with Trent in a matter of hours, if all went smoothly.

She shampooed her hair, then applied conditioner to leave in so her hair would be, according to the bottle, luxuriously silky for her first lesson with Trent.

Now why'd she have to go and think of him, when she barely had full control of her senses as it was, when the pulsating shower head was almost more temptation than she could handle?

She closed her eyes against the spray and tried to block out the mental images that were flooding her brain. It wasn't working. She saw Trent with his shirt off, taut muscles straining over her. Trent with *all* his clothes off, positioned between her legs, his erection about to penetrate her.

The shower spray hit her sensitive breasts and, in spite of herself, she arched her back toward the painful yet pleasant sensation. Her nipples pulled into tight, hard peaks, and she grabbed a bar of soap and started lathering in an attempt to focus on the task at hand.

What she needed was a distraction. She should think about doing her taxes…or waxing her legs…or clipping Eros's claws. But her imagination rebelled just as her hand with the bar of soap slipped between her legs.

They became Trent's hands, rubbing, massaging, slowly coaxing her toward the release she was aching for.

She gasped and sagged back against the tiled shower wall. *Trent, yes, please, I want you…* The throbbing at her core grew until it filled her, then consumed her.

She removed the detachable shower head and brought it down slowly, the pulsing spray almost more than she could stand. When it hit that most sensitive part of her, she cried out, gasping, her heart racing as her pelvic muscles contracted and she found release.

She imagined Trent's hard, wet body pressed against her there in the shower, holding her up against the wall as she caught her breath. He would hold her until she had control of her senses again. And then he would kiss her senseless until they were ready for a second round.

But then she did come to her senses, and it was only her there, alone in the shower, with the cold realization that she'd just gotten a little too friendly with her detachable shower head. She released it from a clutch hold and it fell to the shower floor with a clunk.

Josie shook herself, feeling a little light-headed from the lack of blood flow to her brain. She rinsed the conditioner from her hair and turned off the water. Stepping out to grab a towel, she saw from the bathroom clock radio that she had less than an hour to get to Trent's house.

Less than an hour to mentally prepare herself for her new sexual destiny; less than an hour to calm her nerves enough to follow through; less than an hour to decide exactly what it meant to give a man sex lessons.

IT HADN'T OCCURRED TO Josie until she was standing in Trent's living room how awkward these lessons could be. She was actually going to try to teach the principles of a long-lasting sexual and emotional relationship to the same guy who'd given her the nickname Josie the Tease in high school? What had she been thinking?

"You going to stand there all night in the middle of my living room, or relax and have a seat?"

"I was just wondering, um, where you'd like to get started?"

Trent's trademark mischievous twinkle lit his blue

eyes and he shrugged. "The living room floor works for me, if that's what you prefer."

Josie fingered her folder full of notes, only now realizing how ridiculous it was that she'd thought of using notes for tonight's lesson. How could she expect to seduce a man when she had to refer to an outline?

Was she making a huge mistake? Her pulse quickened and she turned and eyed the door. It wasn't too late to back out. She could find some other way to save the Lovers for Life Center.

"You're not thinking of backing out of our agreement, are you?"

"About that…"

He rose and went to her, stood just inches away as he said, "I need your help. I'm getting tired of the bachelor scene. Someday soon it'll be time for me to settle down, have a real relationship with a woman…start looking toward the future."

"But—"

"I need you, Josie. I've got to learn how to please a woman in the bedroom if I'm ever going to find one that wants to stay with me."

Now, with him so close, her body was warming up. Memories of her shower a short time ago made her cheeks burn as she looked him in the eye. He seemed so truly earnest in his need. How could she not help? Yes, she had to help him, for herself and for him and for his future lovers.

It was time to put all her theoretical knowledge about sex into practice.

She took a deep breath and smiled at Trent. "Well, of course I wasn't thinking of backing out. I was just remembering that I forgot to fill out my questionnaire and bring it along as we'd agreed."

"Forgot, huh?"

"Sorry." She produced an apologetic smile. "Do you have yours ready for me?"

He nodded. "You can finish answering yours orally later."

Oh, great.

His gaze fell to her mouth, and she took that as her cue to get started.

"Every sexual encounter," she began, her voice a little shaky, "should begin with a kiss."

"So you want to check out my technique?"

"Uh, yes, I think that would be prudent."

His lips curved into a sly grin. "Isn't that rushing things a little?"

"Well, not if we're going to get right down to business. No, I don't think it's rushing."

"But isn't great sex based on mutual attraction and affection?"

Okay, he sort of had a point there. But Josie intended to prove that great sex needed only two willing bodies.

"It's good to have both, but in a pinch, plain old sexual attraction will do."

He shrugged. "You're the expert."

She glanced down at her feet, clad in strappy black sandals that she'd thought Trent might find sexy. The vague feeling that he was playing a game with her rose up in her chest. "I prefer to think of myself as an educator, not an expert."

"Whatever you say." His voice was lower now, and he'd lost the mocking grin.

"Okay, then—" she took a step closer to him, putting aside her doubts "—let's start with a kiss."

"I'd hoped we could take this slow, since I seem to have a problem with rushing into sex."

Slow? He wanted to take it slow? Josie wasn't sure she could survive taking it slow. She wasn't sure her shower head could survive.

"But how will I be able to tailor my lessons to your needs, unless I have a complete picture of what your needs are?" There, he couldn't argue with that.

He quirked one eyebrow. "Good point. Okay, I suppose a little kissing won't hurt."

Trent was only inches from her now. That familiar old panic filled her chest, stopped her breathing, froze her in place.

Reality set in. She couldn't kiss Trent, because kissing would lead to so much more. More than she was ready to handle. Not with him. She'd lose control, lose herself, he was too sexy, too gorgeous, too *everything*...

But he had said his girlfriends always left him after they slept together. He wanted her help because he was a boring lover, not a scorching one.

She reached out tentatively and slipped her arms around his neck. Stood on her tiptoes and tilted her face back, bringing her mouth to his. He pulled her close as he settled his lips on hers, and they began to taste, to explore.

He smelled freshly showered, which made her wonder for a moment if he'd had the same kind of shower she'd had, but then the sensation of his lips on hers overtook her and her mind went blank. His tongue caressed hers, coaxing her slowly but surely into a kiss that could burn the fog off of the San Francisco Bay.

Wow. He was a much better kisser than she remembered. She was just settling in to fully enjoy it when he pulled away, took a step back.

"How was that?"

Josie snapped her mouth shut and blinked, struggling

to remember what he might be talking about. "Your technique seems quite satisfactory to me. You've had complaints about your kissing?"

He shrugged, looking a little embarrassed. She realized she'd have to tread very carefully for the next two months not to step on his ego.

"Not the kissing, no. But I haven't had any rave reviews, either."

Josie frowned, doing her best to consider the issue academically when her body was screaming for sex. "There's always room for improvement. And in my experience, practicing is really the best way to improve."

"I'm willing to try anything."

Ah, good. An eager student was just what she needed right now.

"I suppose we should talk about the right timing for a kiss, before we really get into the practicing." She took a seat on the couch and motioned for him to do the same.

"You mean, how early on a date?"

"Not just that, but how frequently during lovemaking. Kissing is an extremely sensual experience for a woman, just as intimate a form of contact as sexual intercourse." She resisted the urge to glance at her folder full of notes.

"So when's the right time for a first kiss?"

"That really depends on the woman, how well you're hitting it off with her, how strong the physical attraction."

His gaze swept over her briefly. "Take us, for instance. Assuming we hadn't just kissed, how soon do you think would be appropriate for us?"

"That's a tough call, since we've known each other forever, and we're not really on a date now."

"But we're attracted to each other, aren't we?"

Josie shifted in her seat. This was even harder than she'd imagined. He was a student asking too many questions, the bane of every ill-prepared teacher's existence. "Yes, I'd say there's some attraction, but I think we should keep our relationship strictly on a student-teacher level."

He shrugged. "Whatever suits you."

"I hope, by the end of our lessons, you'll have developed a sixth sense about the timing of such things." She swallowed, the taste of Trent still lingering, reminding her of what she really wanted to be doing now. "What you need is practice, lots of practice."

"So is that all we're going to do tonight? Kiss?"

"N-no," Josie stuttered., "I'd like to get a full assessment of your current skill level."

"You mean, like a standardized test?"

Josie bit her lip and held back a grin. "I guess you could call it a test, but it won't be multiple choice."

"I wish you'd let me know ahead of time that I'd be tested, so I could have prepared."

"No preparation necessary. This isn't the kind of exam you can study for."

She felt his gaze follow her as she leaned down and unbuckled the ankle strap of one sandal, then the other. She slipped her feet out slowly, hoping her actions looked seductive and not merely routine. From her vantage point, she took note that his own feet, already bare, were strong and tanned and sexy enough to kiss.

If she were so inclined. Which she wasn't. No, she wasn't desperate enough to develop a foot fetish.

Not yet anyway.

Trent cleared his throat, and Josie sat up, a little embarrassed that she'd been ogling his feet.

"Do you want to do it right here on the couch, or in the bedroom?" he asked.

"Where would you normally bring a woman?"

"Depends on what the night calls for. Sometimes things heat up so fast we don't even make it into the house, other times we make it to the floor inside the front door, or on the couch, or the table, or the bathroom, or the bed—"

"I get the picture." This situation had the distinct disadvantage of requiring her to discuss with Trent his having sex with other women.

"With you, I know from experience things can heat up fast," he said.

And fizzle out just as quickly? No, let's don't start talking about the past. Nothing would ruin Josie's chances of getting laid faster than them getting into a debate about her ditching him at Ocean Beach.

"How about you take me through your standard sexual encounter, step by step?"

"Don't you think that'll kill any chance it has of being hot, if I'm talking the whole time?"

"Hmm, good point. How about you make it sexy talk? Could you do that?"

Trent grinned. "I think I can manage."

"Okay, start with this scenario. You and I have just returned from dinner. We've known each other for a couple of weeks, and this is our second date. The first one went well, but I wasn't interested in anything more than a kiss at the door. Tonight, you've invited me up to your place for drinks, and I've been receptive, leading you to believe that we'll have sex."

"You wouldn't be playing the tease, would you?"

"Of course not." Josie shifted her gaze to the wall, wishing he hadn't brought that up. She deserved the label he'd given her, but tonight that was going to change.

It had to change before she went cross-eyed and started growing hair on her palms. Or was that only supposed to happen to guys?

"Then, I'd have to move a little closer to you on the couch, like this." He scooted over until his hip pressed against hers, and the closeness sent a little jolt to her groin.

"Okay, what next?"

"Guess I'd have to ask you if you're thirsty, since I did invite you up for drinks."

She looked at him from the corner of her eye. "I was hoping you'd used drinks as an excuse to get me here and have your way with me."

"Do I look like that kind of guy?"

"Absolutely."

"In that case, I'll have to take things nice and slow. Show you what a gentleman I really am."

No, no. Please not nice and slow. She flashed what she hoped was a wicked smile. "I'm not interested in gentlemen."

"No?" He looked stumped.

Josie took that opportunity to pounce. Literally. She turned and sat herself down right on top of his lap, straddling him, with her dress pushed up her thighs farther than she'd anticipated. An inch higher and he'd be able to tell what color panties she was wearing.

"I thought *I* was leading here."

"Since this is our hypothetical date, I figured it wouldn't hurt for me to throw you a hypothetical curve ball," Josie said.

She shifted her weight forward a bit, and suddenly there was friction between her legs from him. He was pressed against her, so close. His own body was responding, too, she could tell by the growing hardness she felt beneath his jeans. Her insides began to overheat, then melt.

But then that old familiar feeling of dread filled her abdomen, and sweat broke out on her upper lip. She froze, suddenly unsure if she could really go through with what she'd started.

He nodded at her position on his lap. "This isn't hypothetical."

"Oh, right. But you can still show me what you'd do next."

"I guess I'd have to slide my hand up your dress, to see if the rest of you feels as fine as your thigh does."

Josie looked down and saw that his left hand was indeed resting on her thigh. He slowly slid it upward, turning her skin to gooseflesh, until it disappeared under her dress. He paused at her hip and his fingers dipped under the edge of her panties. Oh, so close. Then he stopped, and Josie thought she might scream.

The muscles in her legs twitched, itching to flee.

"This is all wrong," he said.

"What?"

"This. You and me. We can't just hop into bed for our first lesson."

"I *am* supposed to be teaching you how to improve your sex life, right?" And teach she would, if he'd just move his hand a little to the right.

"Not like this." His hand started to move in the wrong direction, back down her thigh.

"Think of it as an assessment. I can't teach you unless I know your current skill level."

Trent shook his head. "Let's do this right, take it slow."

No, he couldn't be saying what she thought he was saying. She was so close, so ready, so desperate to end this dry spell. And she didn't intend her next orgasm to be alone in the shower. It was going to be with Trent, and it was going to be tonight—or was it? The urge to run again was so strong, almost as strong as the urge to get it on. The two forces were battling in her gut, and now with Trent providing such an easy out, her cowardly side was gaining strength.

Could she stay and do the wild thing, or would she just run away again? Josie closed her eyes. When she opened them and caught the way Trent had been watching her when he'd thought she wasn't looking, she knew exactly what she had to do.

4

TRENT WISHED like hell he hadn't chosen to wear jeans tonight, and especially not such a snug-fitting pair. He had a hard-on that was threatening to burst his zipper, and the lack of room for it was proving damned uncomfortable.

He had to get Josie off his lap. Otherwise his plan would be shot. He'd toss it aside in favor of ripping off her dress and making love to her right there on the living room rug. The look of determination in her eyes was downright hypnotic.

And then he felt his zipper slide down.

"Hold it right there," he said as steadily as he could.

"That's exactly what I intend to do," she whispered with a little smile.

"I mean, stop. We're not doing this. I don't even have protection," he lied.

"No problem. There's a box of condoms in my bag."

Damn modern women.

Trent grasped Josie by the waist and lifted her off his lap, then stood and zipped up his jeans. Sweat trickled down the back of his neck. Josie stared up at him, her coffee-brown eyes round and wide.

This wasn't exactly the temptation game he'd had in mind for tonight. He needed a few minutes to cool off, to regain control.

Josie flashed a wicked smile, then stood up next to

him. Her left hand slipped behind her back. Before Trent realized what she was doing, she shrugged the dress off her shoulders and it slid to the floor, forming a puddle at her feet.

But it wasn't her feet he noticed right now. Oh, no. This woman had the power to defeat Superman. Her breasts sat perched in a frilly white push-up bra, the smooth upper halves exposed. It was an offer so tempting he could hardly refuse. And below that a silken stretch of belly led down to a matching pair of white lace panties that allowed a hint of color to show through.

Her hips, the firmly rounded kind found in center-folds, led to a pair of legs he desperately wanted wrapped around him.

Trent clenched his jaw tight, channeling Superman's strength. He wouldn't be defeated.

He just needed to stay focused on his reason for wanting revenge. He needed to remember Ocean Beach....

Before she'd driven off with his underwear, Trent had been thinking maybe Josie was a woman he could settle down with for a few years, have a real relationship with. But those feelings had disappeared the moment she proved she was incapable of having a serious sexual encounter with a man.

"I've got to tell you, you're not exactly acing your test right now," Josie said.

Her gaze remained locked on him as she reached behind her back again and her bra suddenly snapped loose. Next she eased one bra strap, then the other, off her shoulders. When she dropped her arms, the bra fell to the floor on top of her dress.

The sweat spread to his forehead, his upper lip. Damn, it was getting hot in this apartment.

What ever happened to Josie the Tease?

"Your examination methods are questionable at best."

She shrugged, standing almost completely naked in front of him, trying to look undaunted. The hint of color in her cheeks revealed otherwise.

"Challenging students call for unconventional teaching methods," she said almost too casually.

He had to do something, quick.

"It's hot in here, don't you think?" Trent turned and went to the kitchen. Opened the freezer and removed a tray of ice. Cracked it into an empty bowl.

"I'm fine," she said, following him.

He was hyperaware of her every move, and it took all his willpower not to turn and watch how her nearly naked body moved as she walked.

"You sure? You were just looking a little flushed."

What he wanted was to dump the bowl of ice into his boxers, but now was his chance to demonstrate to himself that his self-control was intact. She stood only inches away from him, leaning against the counter.

Josie eyed the bowl of ice. "What are you going to do with that?"

"I'm burning up, and I thought you might be interested in seeing what I can do with an ice cube." He grabbed her wrist before she could slip away, then pinned her against the kitchen counter with his hips.

If she wanted to play games, he was more than willing to play along.

"Oh," she said.

He took a cube from the bowl and licked it, then lowered the ice to her left nipple. On contact her nipple hardened and she gasped softly. He traced one edge of it up the slope of her chest, then along her collarbone to the other side, and down that breast to the other erect nipple.

"Cool enough to put your clothes back on yet?"

Josie closed her eyes and let her head fall back, arching her breast toward him. "No, I'm feeling fine," she whispered. He could feel his self-control slipping. The tension strained him until his hand shook.

He stepped back and let the ice cube travel lower, along her rib cage, then down the center of her belly to her navel, where he traced a wet circle. She contracted her stomach muscles against the cold, but still she stood her ground, seeming to enjoy his torture.

It was getting even hotter in this cramped little kitchen. Even with the windows open to the night air, Trent could feel his shirt growing damp from perspiration. Maybe he was starting to drive her crazy, too, though. Her breathing had gotten shallow, and she kept arching her breasts ever so slightly toward him.

What he would have given to take each round breast into his mouth. Instead, he slid his hand with the ice cube over her panties, down between her legs, where he settled it into that hottest part of her.

Josie gasped, but she must not have been turned off by the cold, because instead of flinching away she pushed herself up onto the counter. Her lush rear end rested on the cold granite, and she spread her legs wide. It was the most tempting invitation he'd ever received.

Sweet heaven.

Trent closed his eyes, steeling himself. He was turning her on as planned, and he couldn't blow it now.

He applied pressure between her legs with the ice cube, then began a slow, circular rhythm, letting it combine with the friction of her panties against her most sensitive spot.

She expelled a ragged moan. "Your score's getting higher by the minute."

The ice cube was quickly melting away to nothing against her heat. Trent grabbed another from the bowl to replace the melting one in his hand. He dared to let his other hand travel up Josie's belly to the curve of her breast. He applied a soft pressure to her nipple, and she moaned again.

Trent groaned inwardly. Damn. Damn, damn, damn. This was a lot harder than he'd imagined. But Josie was nearing climax fast. His torture was almost over.

He quickened the friction between her legs, gave her a bit more pressure, until she'd climbed just to the edge. He could tell by her quickened breathing, the tenseness of her body, that she was about to come.

She was on the brink. And that's when he stopped. Summoning all his strength, he stepped away from her, then took the half-melted ice cube and rubbed it on the back of his neck, cooling himself hardly at all.

"W-what are you doing?"

He produced his most contrite, pained expression, then raked a hand through his hair for effect. "This is all wrong. We shouldn't be getting carried away so fast. I'm sorry."

She expelled a sound halfway between a growl and a screech. "You can't be serious."

"I just want to do this right."

He willed himself not to look at her small brown nipples, still contracted to hard points. But instead his gaze fell on the little wisps of hair around her face, and it took all his remaining willpower not to reach out and tuck those wild strands behind her ear, then kiss away her frustration.

"I appreciate your concern about taking things too fast," she said as if she were talking to an unreasonable two-year-old.

"I'm glad you understand."

"But I thought you agreed to let me lead these lessons whatever way I see fit."

"I will, I will. I just wasn't prepared for us to hop right into bed. Or onto the counter."

"You're the one who asked for *sex* lessons," she said as she stalked back into the living room, her lovely ass in full view.

"I just thought we'd be going over the rest of that questionnaire tonight. I was looking forward to your answers."

She tried to hide her annoyance behind a thin smile. He watched, fascinated, as she went through the motions of putting her bra back on, then her dress.

"Fine," she said when she was dressed again. "I can't wait to see the rest of your answers."

Trent plucked the sheet of paper off of the coffee table, and peered at it as if he didn't remember where they'd left off. "Let's see, looks like we stopped…um, right about here. Yeah, you were just about to describe to me *your* favorite sexual fantasy."

Josie stared at the questionnaire, looking as if she hoped it would spontaneously combust. Her gaze crept up to meet his and she smiled as if she'd just swallowed something foul and wanted to prove she'd enjoyed it.

She sat at one end of the sofa and tucked her legs and feet up underneath her dress. "My favorite sexual fantasy…"

Trent sat one cushion away and propped his feet up

on the coffee table. He couldn't wait to hear this one. "I'm listening."

"Well, this is easy for me. My favorite fantasy is me making love to Brad Pitt." She smiled.

"No fair. That's not a fantasy. That's just naming a celebrity you lust after."

Josie shrugged. "What can I say? I don't have a very active imagination."

Trent frowned. "You mean, you've never once fantasized about slathering me with whipped cream and licking me from head to toe?"

She turned her gaze heavenward. "I'll never tell."

"You have no idea how far you might get with a little dirty talk."

She looked him up and down, perhaps weighing the truth of his statement. "I think I can imagine, based on what just happened in the kitchen."

"Come on, tempt me."

Josie drew her lower lip between her teeth, still watching him. "Okay, but just remember that old saying, be careful what you ask for…"

She couldn't make him any more frustrated than he already was. Could she? *Superman, think Superman.*

Trent stretched out full-length and put his hands behind his head, mentally prepared to leap over tall buildings in a single bound.

"I'm alone in my office, working late at night," she began. "I look out the window, and I see a lone man in the building across from me. He's in his apartment, wearing nothing but a pair of jeans, and he's leaning against the window, cooling himself in the night air, and watching me."

She paused.

"What next?"

"Are you sure you want to hear this?"

"Absolutely positive."

"Our eyes meet and there's this connection. I start undressing, slowly, making a show of it."

"Who is this guy? Someone you know?"

She chewed her lip for a moment. "We pass on the street. Say hi at the newsstand. Maybe see each other in the grocery store or the deli."

Interesting. If she was making all this up for Trent's benefit, she was doing a damned good acting job. But he'd bet money this was the real deal, one of her most secret fantasies.

"I undress down to my bra and panties, and I'm so turned on, I start touching myself. I touch my breasts, between my legs…"

"What does the guy do?"

"I have my eyes closed for a while, and then I hear a knock at the door. I know it's him, but I say nothing, and he comes in."

"You're still touching yourself?"

"I stop when he knocks on the door. I'm sitting on top of my desk, waiting for him. He comes in and, without saying a word to each other, we make love there on the desk."

"What happens after? Do you ever speak to him?" Trent asked, aware that his own voice sounded slightly strained.

He couldn't help imagining himself pleasuring Josie there in the darkened office, finding inventive uses for ordinary office supplies.

"I don't know. The fantasy never goes all the way to the end." She blushed but didn't look away from him.

"Because you always come first?" he asked, cursing

himself as the words rolled off his tongue. More sweat ran down the back of his neck.

"Mmm-hmm," she said, and Trent knew then that he'd gotten in too deep.

HIS FINGERS, his tongue, were everywhere. Touching, exploring, pleasuring, driving her out of her mind.

"Oh, Trent. Mmm, oh, yes! Trent, please, touch me there—"

The phone rang and Josie tried to ignore it, focusing on the feel of Trent's tongue probing between her legs. He seemed not to hear the incessant ringing. He kept coaxing her to the brink of orgasm, then pulling back, again and again. Driving her mad. But the phone, it wouldn't stop—

Josie was jolted awake by the sound of the ringing phone on her nightstand. She looked around, disoriented by her dream and its sudden interruption. She was soaking wet in her nightshirt, and the sheets were twisted around her legs. She banned the erotic images of Trent from her mind and grabbed the receiver.

Just as she mumbled "Hello?" she caught a glimpse of the clock and saw that it was three in the morning. It had to be her mother, calling in the middle of the next day by Czech time and not caring one bit that she was waking Josie.

"Hello, Josephine. Sleeping alone, I bet."

"Yeah, I just sent home that wrestling team a few hours ago."

Her mother laughed. She was the only mother on earth, as far as Josie knew, who'd laugh at her daughter's joke about group sex with an entire sports team. Josie had given up wishing she had the kind of mom who baked cookies and complained about wanting grandchildren.

"How's the center doing?"

Josie pushed herself up in bed and leaned against the headboard, wide awake now. She had been avoiding telling her mother about how close the business was to utter failure. "Not good."

"You can save it, I'm sure. That's why I asked you to run it for me."

Josie had the feeling her mother's request was motivated by something more than she was letting on. She was normally a shrewd businesswoman—or so Josie had thought until she'd seen what a mess the center's finances were in—and her actions just didn't add up.

"The rent is two months late, and I can't pay it."

"Oh, don't worry about that. Trent O'Reilly is as understanding as he is gorgeous. If you had any sense at all you'd make him forget all about those rent payments."

Josie blinked at how close to the truth her mother was. "Right, Mom. Maybe I should just trade sex to solve the center's financial problems."

"Whatever you want to do, dear." She said it in a way that let Josie know she'd lost interest in the subject.

"What's on your mind?" Josie asked as she suppressed a yawn.

"Oh, it's Peter. I'm afraid things aren't working out so well between us."

"What's wrong?"

"Writer's block. He's had it ever since I moved in with him. The poor thing sits staring at his computer all day without typing a word."

"Hmm."

"I think it's the sex. He's using his creative energy

in bed at night, and I'm leaving him a bit too satisfied, if you know what I mean.''

Josie wished she didn't. The last thing she wanted to picture was her mother in bed with a man twenty years younger than her—or any man at all, actually. But there it was, the image invading her head and chasing away the last remnants of her Trent dream. She was wide awake now.

"Are you thinking of coming home?" Josie asked, not sure which answer she wanted to hear.

"Don't be ridiculous. And leave Prague? This city is to die for. Actually I'm thinking of withholding sex from Peter until he finishes his novel.''

"Hmm.''

"I'm just not sure *I* can tolerate that option. I have needs, too, you know.''

"Wish I didn't,'' Josie muttered away from the receiver.

Her mother either didn't hear or ignored it.

"Or maybe I'll let him pleasure me, but I won't touch him. Oohh, that could be fun.''

"Did you call me at 3:00 a.m. to tell me this?''

"Oh, I almost forgot. I'm calling because I need you to take Eros to the vet for his yearly checkup. I was just looking in my appointment book and saw that his vet visit is scheduled for this Wednesday at eleven…''

Her mother continued to talk, but Josie didn't hear her. She sat bolt upright in bed, her pulse racing. Eros! When was the last time she'd seen him?

Think, Josie. Think.

Not since early yesterday evening, before her "Great Sex After Sixty'' seminar. She must have been so distracted by thoughts of Trent that she'd failed to notice that he hadn't shown up for dinner, or breakfast, or dinner again.

Oh, for heaven's sake, she would never forgive herself if something had happened to that cat. As poorly as she got along with Eros, it was her job to take care of him, and she'd failed. Her mother would never forgive her, either.

When Rafaela finally stopped talking, Josie said a hurried goodbye and jumped out of bed, grabbed the jeans on a nearby chair and tugged them on. Her nightshirt was a cotton-and-lace camisole, still damp from her heated dreams, but it would have to do for street wear for now.

Where could the cat be? He liked to wander, but he faithfully showed up for mealtimes without fail. He was staying at Lovers for Life while her mother was gone, because Josie was allergic and couldn't keep him in her apartment, but she definitely hadn't seen him there in the past day and a half.

Horrific images flashed through her mind—all the awful things that could happen to the poor animal if he'd wandered outside and then couldn't get back in. She had to get to the center immediately to start looking for him. Maybe he'd just gotten shut in a storage closet. Or maybe not. But she couldn't rest as long as she was worrying about him.

She jammed her feet into a pair of sandals and headed for the front door, grabbing her purse along the way. When she got to the door, she remembered that she didn't have a key to the center, not since Erika had lost hers and borrowed Josie's to open up in the mornings.

Great, now she'd have to wait until morning. Or call Erika and wake her up. She gnawed her lip for a few moments before making up her mind. She'd call Erika and apologize profusely for the rude late-night interruption.

She grabbed the cordless phone from an end table and dialed. But the phone rang and rang, and rang some more. No answer at Erika's house.

Josie let out a frustrated roar and fumbled with the disconnect button, then slammed the phone on the wall a few times for emphasis.

Okay, what could she do now? She could go out and search the area around the center for Eros, but that was definitely not safe. She could try to jimmy the lock at the center, but she hadn't a clue how to go about doing it. Or…

She could call the landlord and ask for his key. The landlord she'd been having lurid dreams about moments ago. The idea tumbled around in her head for a few minutes before she decided she would do it. The alternative, waiting until morning, could mean the difference between life and death for Eros, and she had to do all she could to find him and keep him safe.

If it wasn't too late already.

That thought sent her fumbling through her address book for Trent's number and, without stopping to reconsider, she punched the numbers into her phone. It rang once, twice, three times before she heard a sleepy "Hello?" on the other end of the line.

"Trent, it's me, Josie. I'm sorry to be calling so late."

"Josie?"

She heard fumbling, the sound of the phone being jostled around, and she imagined him sitting up in bed. He was probably naked from the waist up and the sheet probably pooled in his lap, barely covering his—

"What are you calling for?" he asked, sounding both concerned and annoyed.

"I need to get into the center immediately, and I don't have a key. Can I come by and get yours?"

"Is something wrong?"

"It's my mother's cat. He's staying there at the center, but I just realized I haven't seen him in almost two days. I need to look for him."

A frustrated sigh came across the line. "He's a cat. They wander. It's no cause for an early morning search and rescue mission."

"Eros always shows up for meals, and he's not even supposed to be going outside while my mother is gone. She's afraid he'll wander off and not come back without her around."

"And you let him out anyway?"

"Well, no. But sometimes he darts outside when people come in and out the door. He always comes back, though, but I haven't seen him, I just realized."

"You were up at three in the morning thinking about your mother's cat?"

No, I was in bed dreaming of making love to you.

Josie felt her cheeks burning. "Rafaela called and woke me up. She doesn't get this whole different-time-zones concept." She heard his breathing on the other end of the line and somehow it felt intimate, as if he were right there. Suddenly the thought of the two of them, on the phone while the rest of the city slept, was turning her thighs to jelly. She crossed her legs, but the friction of the denim against her crotch was too much so she uncrossed them and stood.

"Give me directions to your place. I'll come by and pick you up."

"Trent, that's not necessary. I can come get the key."

"Out of the question. It's not safe to be out looking for a cat at this time of night. If you want my key, you get my help, too."

His offer was generous, but he sounded none too thrilled about the proposition. Still, he was right. She wouldn't feel safe in the neighborhood around the center this late.

After giving him directions to her apartment, she hung up the phone and paced the living room floor. Then a glimpse of her disheveled appearance in the entryway mirror gave her pause. Her wavy hair had been transformed into its usual nighttime bushy do by sleep, and her eyes were puffy and tired. Oh, dear. She couldn't greet Trent looking like one of the Muppets.

Josie hurried to the bathroom and winced as she switched on the bright light. Egad. It would take him fifteen minutes, twenty tops, to get to her place from where he lived. And in the mirror she saw an hour's worth of work. She dumped her makeup bag on the counter and grabbed the lipstick. She had turned her lips halfway Passionate Pink when she realized the absurdity of putting on makeup for Trent at this hour.

If he arrived to find her made up, he'd know she'd done it to impress him, and that wouldn't do. Trent would laugh at such obvious tactics. No, this situation called for the subtle approach.

She scowled and grabbed a tissue to wipe off the lipstick. A little concealer under the eyes, the ever-so-slightest remnant of lipstick to color her lips, a few strokes of mascara to darken the lashes, and she could look a little more like she'd just rolled out of bed, without looking *like she'd just rolled out of bed*.

That left her hair to contend with. She picked up the nearest brush, but then thought better of it. Instead she ran her fingers through her mop of curls until they tumbled in a more desirable manner than every which way, and she could almost envision herself as a slightly nerdy version of one of those just-awakened catalog models, showing off the latest summer pajamas.

Uh-oh. Speaking of pajamas, her own PJ top was a little more revealing than she'd realized. She squinted at the lace and confirmed that yes, indeed, the edges of her areolas showed through. Since she wasn't wearing a bra, her breasts bobbed and swayed with every movement, and her nipples stood at attention from the cool night air seeping in the bathroom window.

This wouldn't do at all... Or would it? She wanted to seduce Trent, didn't she? And what better way was there than to provide a little enticement, a hint of pleasures to come?

Smiling, she went into the hallway, dug an old denim jacket out of the closet, and shrugged it on over her camisole. The effect was perfect, hiding just enough to keep her modesty intact, but if he looked closely, he'd get quite a show.

A soft rap at the door startled her back to reality, and her mind immediately focused on Eros. That poor, ornery cat... Where the heck was he?

A quick look through the peephole revealed Trent on the other side of the door, looking every bit as rumpled and tired as herself. She wondered if, after their steamy lesson, his dreams had been as erotic as hers. She opened the door and gave him an apologetic smile.

"I owe you for this," she whispered, stepping out into the hallway.

The old house she lived in had been converted into four tiny apartments. Her neighbors could hear just about everything, and while several of them were night owls, it wouldn't win her any friends to make unnecessary noise at three-thirty in the morning.

"I'll add it to your tab."

Josie locked the door and when she turned to face Trent, the images of her dream came back. She felt her pulse quicken.

"I guess we both should drive," she offered, to take her mind off of more erotic thoughts.

"No way am I driving with you right in front of or behind me," he said, matching her own hushed tones. "You can ride with me. I'll bring you back after."

"There's nothing wrong with my driving."

"Uh-huh. You're riding with me."

"And if we find Eros, you'll let the cat inside your precious car?"

"Absolutely. Eros and I are buddies from way back."

"It figures."

Trent followed her down the front steps and then walked ahead of her to open the passenger side door of his car. Once they were both settled inside and buckled in, he took off in the direction of Lovers for Life.

Josie hoped their riding together didn't remind him of the last time they'd been in a car together, when she'd bailed on him at the beach. If he ever questioned her about that night, she had no idea how she'd explain her behavior. She had a sexual hang-up that not even she could understand, let alone offer any reasonable excuses for.

But with Trent she was determined to conquer her fear. Soon, very soon, she'd be having wild, passionate sex with the man of her fantasies.

This time, she wouldn't run away.

Their first lesson hadn't exactly been a success. She may have flat-out failed to seduce Trent, but she was so pleased with the sexual boldness she'd managed to display, she couldn't count the entire night a failure. Even more important, she'd never backed down from him. She'd harnessed her fear and turned it into the courage she needed, and she was quite sure, given enough time, she'd have Trent as her lover.

Her future lover yawned noisily. "You're being awful quiet over there. Don't fall asleep on me."

"Trust me, if I could sleep right now, I wouldn't have called you."

"Got a plan for how we'll find the cat?"

"I need to search the center first, and if he's not there, I guess we'll have to grab a can of Fancy Feast and start combing the neighborhood."

"Does your mother know he's missing?"

"No, and she can't find out. She'll have a conniption."

"Ah, so I've got a little information on you now."

"I hope you can be kind enough not to use it against me."

He grinned as he pulled the Porsche into an empty space in front of the center. "We'll just have to see about that."

She ignored his taunt, all her energy focused on finding Eros.

Trent got out of the car and was on his way to her side to open the door when she opened it herself and climbed out.

"You're supposed to let the gentleman do that, you know."

"We're not on a date. You don't have to be polite."

He opened his mouth to speak but the words must have frozen in his throat, because just at that moment his gaze dropped to her chest. Even by the dim light of a nearby street lamp, he must have been able to see exactly what she'd intended him to see.

She repressed a satisfied smile and pretended not to notice his staring.

"You shouldn't be out in public like that."

"It's just you and me."

He took a step closer and pinned her in place with his gaze. "You wouldn't be playing the tease with me, would you?"

"Me? Teasing you? After what you did to me last night?" She smiled and slid one hand up his chest. "You bet I am."

5

JOSIE WAS CLOSE ENOUGH that Trent could see the tiny bumps on her skin from the chill in the night air—and the far more obvious bumps created by her hardened nipples. It took all his willpower not to reach out and touch her there, to trace the dark circles visible through the lace on her top, to pull her close and do things to her he knew would take the chill away.

"That cat had better be missing for real," Trent muttered.

Her expression changed instantly from seductive to worried. "Of course he is. I wouldn't fake something like that. Unlock the building so I can look inside."

Trent dug the key out of his pocket and went to the front door, noting the lack of a cat in the center's front window. Eros was almost always there, watching outside.

Josie called, "Eros? Here, Eros! Dinnertime, kitty-kitty-kitty!" Her footsteps closed in behind him. "I hope he's just lying low somewhere pouting because I bought him the wrong kind of food."

The concern in her voice touched him. He'd never known she had a soft spot for animals. As a kid she'd always cowered away from Trent's childhood mutt. Granted, Amos had been a huge dog, but most of the neighborhood kids had run up to pet the harmless beast, while Josie had acted as if at any moment he might decide she was dinner.

They entered the center and switched on some lights, calling for Eros as they moved toward the back.

"I'll get the Fancy Feast ready while you keep looking for him," Josie called.

Trent went into Rafaela's office and switched on a light. "Here, kitty-kitty," he said halfheartedly, sure the cat wasn't going to be found anywhere inside.

The photographs on the bookshelves behind the desk caught Trent's eye. He'd never noticed them before, so he slipped past the desk and studied the images framed in artsy sculpted metal. Rafaela, much younger, with a blond man that bore a striking resemblance to Josie, with his even features and deep brown eyes.

The next photo showed Rafaela, slightly older, her arm draped around the neck of a deeply tanned pretty-boy in a leather jacket. He skimmed the photos, which seemed to all be Rafaela with various boyfriends. The last one showed her with a tall, thin guy sporting a ponytail down his back. He was roughly half her age. This one must have been Peter, the latest male bimbo in her vast collection.

Trent shook his head and ducked back out of the office, switching off the light as he went. He'd always felt a little sorry for Josie, growing up with a mother so different from the norm. But, hey, this was San Francisco, where few people fit an all-American mold of normalcy. Still, that long line of men marching in and out of her life must have scarred her.

Josie had opened the back door of the building and was standing in the alley with a plate of cat food so rank Trent could smell it from where he stood. She was calling for Eros, with no success.

As Trent neared a closet, an odd feeling caused him to pause. He opened the closet door and there sat the missing cat, scowling at him as if Trent himself were responsible for his getting shut in there.

"Hey, little guy, you could have at least howled for us."

In response, Eros flicked his tail and stalked out of the closet.

"Found him!" Trent called toward the back.

"Thank goodness." Josie came running inside and dropped to her knees next to Eros, who sat licking one paw.

As Josie reached out to stroke his knobby black head, she expelled a string of dainty girl sneezes. Eros swatted at her hand, then bit her. Trent couldn't help laughing.

"Looks like he blames you for his confinement."

"He blames me for everything. He must have slipped into the closet yesterday while Erika was vacuuming between afternoon and evening classes. He hates the vacuum cleaner."

She rubbed the spot on her hand where he'd bit her.

"Eros is a perceptive cat. I think he knows you're not to be trusted with the opposite sex."

Josie looked at Trent sideways, her tousled hair falling over one eye in a way that made him think of lazy Saturday-morning sex.

"Me? Not to be trusted?"

He twitched his eyebrows, crossed his arms over his chest. "That's right."

"You're not still mad about Ocean Beach."

This was the first time the subject of that ill-fated night had come up in the three years since it happened. Trent was almost surprised to hear her acknowledge it, finally.

"You are, aren't you? I owe you an apology."

He had to admit, she looked sufficiently ashamed, but that didn't change the fact that she'd ditched him.

"I had to hitchhike home that night. Without my underwear," he added.

"I didn't mean to keep them. They were under the passenger seat where I couldn't see them."

"Uh-huh."

"Really!" She blushed and there suddenly seemed nothing else to say about the matter.

They stood staring at each other, as the awkward silence grew longer and longer. Trent scrambled to think of all the things he'd envisioned himself saying to her when he finally got the chance. And now his memory was letting him down.

Josie finally said, "Listen, I just need to fill up Eros's dry food bowl and then we can go. I'm sorry to drag you out at this hour for a false alarm."

"Don't think you're going to end this conversation that easily." *Think. Think, man, think!*

He followed Josie into the back room where she filled the cat's food and water bowls. Eros sat watching her every move, and when she finished he strolled over to the bowl, gave it a tentative sniff, and then attempted to bury it with one paw as if it was last week's kitty litter.

Trent positioned himself in the middle of the doorway, leaving her no escape route.

Josie held up her palms in surrender. "What can I do to make it up to you?"

He grinned. "I like this new submissive attitude."

"Don't press your luck."

What could she do, indeed? An image of the office

popped into his head. A large desk, an executive chair, an overstuffed couch… Hmm.

No, no, no, no, no. His body couldn't take another round of what he'd already endured with Josie so soon. He needed time to recover, to build up an iron will to fight her sexual charms.

But then his libido took over and he blurted, "I've got an office fantasy of my own, you know."

"You do?"

Damn it! Why couldn't he have just kept his mouth shut?

The spark of interest in her eyes was all the encouragement his overtaxed libido needed.

"Come here." He motioned her toward the office and she followed him.

He turned on a table lamp, his pulse racing as if he'd just gotten a girl alone for the first time. "Imagine this. You're the high-powered executive and I'm the nervous young intern."

Her jaw sagged for a moment, and then she recovered. A look of pure mischief passed over her face. He'd hooked her.

His brain was still sending weak signals—*Run, run, run!*—but his dick had taken over all decision-making processes for the time being.

She repressed a smile. "That would hardly be appropriate, considering our professional arrangement."

"Just last night you weren't so concerned with behaving appropriately."

"And you were harping about how you didn't want to move too fast. What gives?"

Trent shrugged and tried to appear contrite. "Let's just say I haven't gotten much sleep since our first lesson."

She beamed. "Sorry to hear that."

"Yeah, right. How about you consider this a bonus lesson?"

"How is acting out your favorite office fantasy a lesson?"

Trent did his best to look uncomfortable. He shifted his gaze to the floor, rubbed the back of his neck. "I've never been any good at role-playing in the bedroom. I've heard it can add, um, interest, or whatever."

Josie took a deep breath. "Well, that's true. In a committed relationship, sometimes couples have to get creative in order to keep things fresh in the bedroom."

Trent plastered on an earnest expression. "Then you'll be helping me out."

He went to her, stood close enough that he could remove that scrap of a top she wore with one good tug.

For several moments she was silent, watching him, and then she began. "Have a seat, Mr....O'Reilly, is it? Tell me what's brought you to my office."

He sat, forcing himself not to think erotic thoughts. If he got too turned on by this game, he'd never be able to leave Josie hot and bothered again.

"I have a problem, Ms. Marcus," he started tentatively. "I'm sorry to turn to you with it, but I didn't know where else to go."

She shrugged off her denim jacket, giving him a prime view of her barely concealed breasts and creamy satin shoulders.

"I'm a busy woman, Mr. O'Reilly. I hope you can keep this short."

"Oh, no, I'm sorry, ma'am. This could take a while."

Her eyes dilated and she sat on the edge of the desk, looking a little unsteady on her feet. "How long?"

"Possibly all night."

"Tell me what the problem is."

"It's...you, Ms. Marcus. I just can't focus on work while you're walking around the office in that revealing top."

She licked her lower lip. "Hmm. I think I know the solution to that."

"Yes?"

"Come here, please."

He stood and went to her, his erection already growing. His pulse raced the way a wild animal's must when it was trapped by a predator. The only difference was, Trent was the hunted and he didn't even have the sense to run.

She took his hand and pulled him to her. "It's time for your real internship to begin."

Trent groaned as she slid one hand between them, cupped his cock in her palm, and squeezed gently through his jeans. When she began to work the zipper, he stepped back.

A warning bell had sounded in his head, but his ability to heed common sense was long gone.

"Ms. Marcus, if you don't mind, I'd like to show you what I've learned since coming here to your company."

Josie smiled slyly. "I'm always interested in our up-and-coming talent."

Trent winced at her pun, but not for long. His gaze caught on a glint of gold metal. He plucked a letter opener off the desk, then slipped it under one strap of Josie's camisole and tugged the bit of lace over her shoulder, baring her breast. Her nipple stood at attention, begging to be kissed, and it was an invitation he could no longer resist. He leaned over and tasted it, teasing with his tongue, sucking gently.

Oh, God, he was in trouble. Deep, deep trouble.

She arched her back, and her breath quickened as Trent traced her unexposed nipple with the side of the letter opener, and used his other hand to dip between her legs.

"May I show you what else I've learned, Ms. Marcus?"

"Please do," she whispered.

He unfastened her jeans, pulled her up to a standing position, then tugged them down over her thighs. What was left in his way was a pair of black satin panties. Yeah, he was a goner. His whole damn revenge plan was out the window.

But when he turned her around to illustrate the many interesting uses of the common executive chair, Josie stiffened. His hands paused midstroke on her waist and he followed her line of vision to the display of Rafaela and her many boy bimbos.

"Oh, yuck," Josie said. "Yuck, yuck, yuck."

"How about I turn off the light?"

She shuddered, then turned to face him. Her complexion had paled. "I'm sorry, but... Ugh, seeing my mom there, and those guys... It just killed the mood."

Trent started to protest, then caught himself. Common sense took hold and he realized how close he'd just come to ruining his chance at revenge.

"Completely understandable." He trailed his fingers along her rib cage, then pulled her close. "This probably isn't the right time, anyway. I mean, I was letting my libido do the decision-making."

Josie sank onto the edge of the desk, crossing her arms over her chest. "Why does my mother have to shack up with guys the same age as her own daughter?"

Trent shook his head and rubbed her arm. "Parents—

what do we do with them? You know, my dad dates women my age, too. Maybe he and your mother should get together and swap jailbait stories.''

Josie flashed a half smile. She stood up from the desk and retrieved her jacket from the floor, then shrugged it on. ''Sorry to keep you out so late. We should get going.''

Trent nodded and followed her as she switched off lights and headed for the front door. Outside, he locked up the building and turned to find Josie staring up at the Lovers for Life Center sign above the door, looking wistful.

''I can't believe how long this place has been around,'' she said.

''What's it been? Twenty years?''

''Twenty-two this fall. It just doesn't make any sense—all the work Mom put into this place, and then she just up and leaves it in near financial ruin, all for some bimbo guy.''

Trent frowned. ''It does seem odd, even for Rafaela.''

Josie blinked, and if he wasn't mistaken, Trent could have sworn he saw some extra dampness in her eyes.

''I just don't want to see this place close. I used to hate it when I was a kid, but now—I know it sounds corny—it feels like a part of me would be lost if it shuts down.''

Guilt stabbed Trent in the gut. Josie had no idea how close she really was to the possibility of seeing the business close for good. The Lovers for Life Center's lease was up in two more months and before she'd left for Prague Rafaela had mentioned that she might not want to renew it. She'd also sworn Trent to secrecy on the subject.

The knowledge that one of his adjoining properties might soon become vacant, along with a tempting offer from the chain bookstore MegaBooks, presented Trent with a difficult decision to make. MegaBooks was willing to pay top dollar for the side-by-side properties where Lovers for Life and Extreme Sports were located, so that the bookstore chain could knock down the two buildings to build one of its monolithic stores right in the heart of an otherwise unique business district. Trent had to decide whether he was ready to close Extreme Sports and move to Tahoe, as he'd been halfheartedly planning.

To complicate matters, in the past, the local neighborhood association had vehemently fought large business chains moving in, and Trent himself wasn't even sure he could stomach seeing two locally owned businesses replaced by a MegaBooks. But the money they were offering was very, very good.

He couldn't dwell on that right now, not with Josie looking so forlorn. "Do you think your mother is trying to teach you some kind of lesson or something, putting you in this situation?"

Josie shrugged, and they began walking toward Trent's car. "That thought has occurred to me. But what's the lesson? How not to save a dying business?"

"Knowing Rafaela, it would never be something so obvious. Maybe she's trying to force you and the cat to get along."

They both laughed, while Trent opened the car door for Josie and she climbed in. He closed the door and as he headed to the driver's side of the car, the stabbing feeling in his gut turned to a dull ache. It wasn't just the thought of selling the properties and leaving San

Francisco that nagged at him—it was the whole idea of giving up his connection to Josie for good.

And if the sex lessons weren't enough to keep him tossing in his bed at night, that thought sure as hell was.

JOSIE SUPPRESSED A YAWN, adjusted her black leather corset, and peeked at the clock over the rim of her reading glasses. It was only six thirty-five, which meant she had roughly three hours and twenty-five minutes before she could go home to try to catch up on the sleep she'd lost the night before while looking for Eros and replaying her near-miss in the office with Trent in her head.

She absolutely was *not* going to think about that embarrassing scene again right now.

One of the attendees of tonight's seminar, Introductory S&M, was explaining his hesitance to try bondage. Josie tried to pay attention, but in those rare moments when she managed to force all sexual thoughts of Trent from her mind, the myriad problems at the center took over. Aside from the late rent, there were also all the other late bills. There was Erika's salary to pay—one thing Josie wouldn't let slide, no matter what—and there was Josie's own salary. She'd cut her paychecks down to the bare minimum, but that still didn't leave much cash to pick up the slack elsewhere.

But then thoughts of her financial woes inevitably led her on a mental path back to Trent and their scandalous arrangement. After two nights in a row of sexual frustration, Josie was a mess on the job. Aside from her inability to focus, and her constant thoughts of sex, she'd begun to think of everything in terms of their future sex lessons. Even now, she was imagining how she might incorporate her newly learned dominatrix skills into a lesson for Trent.

"…and that's a big part of my problem," Mr. Vowell was saying. He paused and stared at Josie, awaiting her response.

Too bad she hadn't been listening. Josie tried to focus her brain on the present. She opened her mouth and mentally commanded a response to appear. "Your penisship is long."

"Excuse me, Ms. Marcus? My penis *what* is long?"

Josie blinked. Her cheeks burned. "Did I just say—er, I meant to say your *partnership* is *strong*."

Mr. and Mrs. Vowell stared at her, mouths simultaneously agape. The rest of the class was silent, probably wondering what they were doing in a seminar taught by a bumbling imbecile.

"I'm so sorry," Josie said, covering her face with her hands for a moment. "I got very little sleep last night. I'm afraid it's adversely affecting me. Please, let's continue."

She didn't want to be here now, leading this silly seminar, dressed up like a dominatrix. Aside from the fact that she had no experience in the subject matter, and that her bustier was about to cut off the oxygen supply to her brain, she was a total mess after last night.

But at the last minute she'd decided she couldn't afford to cancel the seminar, regardless of the fact that there was no instructor.

The rest of the group seemed undaunted by Josie's slip-up. They simply sat in their circle, waiting for Mr. Vowell to continue discussing his reservations about trying bondage. There really was no need to be embarrassed about making a penis slip among people who were comfortable talking to strangers about how hard their spouses like to be whipped on the fanny. But still…

"Please go ahead, Mr. Vowell. You were discussing your fear of disrupting the trust in your relationship."

"Yes, and I agree with you, Amelia and I do have a strong partnership. But I just think it might be violated if we start tying each other up and engaging in spankings."

His wife seemed to have regained her composure for the moment. "But I want to be tied up! I don't see how it's violating anything if we're both consenting adults."

Josie intervened when Mr. Vowell failed to respond. "Could it be that you have some issues surrounding sadomasochism? Perhaps it doesn't fit your idea of what respectable married people do?"

He nodded, giving the matter some thought. "Yes, I suppose that's true. I mean, we're parents, for goodness sake! We're not supposed to be gallivanting around the bedroom with whips and chains."

Mrs. Vowell looked to Josie for help.

"It's up to both of you to decide what is acceptable within the boundaries of your marriage. This is an issue I think you should discuss in further depth privately, or I'd be happy to hold a private session with you if you think it would help."

The rest of the class looked relieved that they would be moving on from Mr. Vowell's sexual hang-ups and getting back to the subject at hand.

"Could we have a demonstration of what all these tools are for?" Ellen Taylor, a demure thirty-something R.N., asked as she held up a small mace from the table full of implements in the center of the room.

Josie cringed. She'd spent the morning sorting through the S&M paraphernalia Erika had found in a box in the storage room. Between the two of them they'd figured out what most of the tools were used for, but a few items had left them perplexed. There was that doohickey with all the straps and buckles…and that stick with the *thing* on the end of it.

"Of course, we'll have time for that." Panic seized her chest—or maybe it was just the corset—and she knew she needed to take a quick breather. Josie stood. "I'm going to step out of the class for a few moments. While I'm gone, sort through the tools on the table, and feel free to discuss them amongst yourselves."

She hurried out of the room, hoping her rear end didn't look too atrocious in the skin-tight black leather miniskirt, and paused in the empty hallway to take a deep breath. The corset bound her so tightly that she couldn't fill her lungs all the way up, couldn't quite breathe the way she normally did.

The sound of sandals slapping against wood alerted her to Erika's approach. She turned and forced a smile.

"You should at least take your glasses off. Dominatrixes don't wear wire-rimmed frames," Erika said, inspecting Josie from head to toe.

"The cat dander in the building has my eyes all itchy. I can't wear contacts right now."

Erika reached up and removed the frames. "You only wear these for reading, right?"

"Right, and I need to read my class notes." Josie reached for the glasses, and Erika hid them behind her back.

"You have a visitor out front. Normally I wouldn't interrupt class to tell you, but seeing as how you're dressed up like you are, I was going to pop in and let you know—"

"Who is it?"

"Hunk-a-licious from next door."

"Trent?"

"He says he left something in your office last night?" Erika raised an eyebrow.

Last night. Josie had to somehow keep her mind off of the events that had led to her confusing words like "partnership" and "penis."

"Let him see you like this and he'll be putty in your hands. I'll just send him on back." Erika turned and headed toward the lobby, but Josie grabbed her arm.

"Wait!"

"Hey, I've got it—I'll tell him you need some help with a class, and he can be your volunteer whipping boy."

Josie giggled at the idea and then sobered. Maybe Erika had something there. She'd intended to ask for a volunteer from the class to help her, but it would be far more effective to use someone whose wife wasn't sitting a few feet away.

"Send him back here."

Erika flashed an alligator grin, then hurried to the lobby. A moment later Trent appeared in the hallway. As he approached he took in Josie's attire, surveying her head to toe, and back up again.

"Damn, I came dressed all wrong."

"I need your help." She grasped his hand. "I'm doing a demonstration in this seminar, and I need an assistant."

"Isn't that Erika's job?"

"A *male* assistant."

"What do I have to do?"

"Nothing really. Just sit there and look cute."

"I thought I wasn't allowed to drop in on your classes anymore."

"I'm making an exception."

A slow smile spread across his lips. "Honey, wear that outfit and I'll go wherever you want."

Josie smiled. "Good. Come on in."

She led Trent to the chair where she'd previously been sitting, and he took a seat.

"Everyone, I'd like you to meet my partner for the evening, Trent. He'll be helping me in a demonstration."

Trent eyed the table, with its assortment of leather-and-metal implements, then shot Josie a warning look. She ignored him. Now was the time to adopt her dominatrix persona. One of the goals of the class was to give participants concrete ways to get started in S&M. The inexperienced in the class needed a clear idea of how to behave in the beginning, so that they could build their confidence and become more adventurous.

Josie herself had to rely on the how-to video she'd watched and taken notes on a few hours before, in place of any real experience at whipping men into submission. She picked up her class notes and tried to scan them one last time, but her eyes couldn't focus on the jumble of letters. So much for preparation.

"It's really up to you as a couple to decide who plays the dominant role and who will be the submissive. Some couples prefer to switch roles back and forth."

She went to the table and selected a black strip of cloth, a pair of handcuffs and a whip. When she turned to Trent, she could have sworn she'd caught him staring at her with raw, unabashed lust. Maybe she was a more convincing dominatrix than she thought.

Recalling the posture of the woman in the video, Josie puffed up her chest as best she could and assumed an authoritative stance, her feet spread wide apart. She pulled back the whip and, just as she'd practiced with Erika earlier, cracked it in the air near Trent's chair.

Except, instead of cracking in the air, she managed to hit Trent's thigh.

"Ouch!" He raised his hands in a gesture of surrender.

Okay, minor setback. She'd just act as though she'd meant to whip him. This was a lesson in domination and submission, after all, right? She just had to think of what a real dominatrix would say.

"Shut up, Slave Boy. I'll let you know when it's your turn to speak."

6

SLAVE BOY? Since when had he earned that title?

Josie gave him a private look that pleaded for him to play along. Okay, he would, for the sake of curiosity. He could hardly wait to see what she'd do next.

He mentally slipped into his new slave-boy persona. "Yes, Mistress. I'm sorry for being such a bad slave. I deserve to be punished."

Trent winced at the lingering pain in his thigh. Just what he needed—a clumsy dominatrix. Only when Josie headed toward him with handcuffs did he realize what a fool's mission he was on. He'd dropped by the center in the guise of looking for his wallet, which wasn't really lost at all, but the sight of Josie in that shiny black latex getup had distracted him from his plan.

He'd spent last night wide awake, just as he'd feared he would, agonizing over that feeling in his gut that he'd let emotions get involved in his relationship with Josie.

So tonight he'd decided he would drop by, spend some time hanging out with her, just long enough to convince himself that he'd been dead wrong last night; that his attraction to her was purely sexual.

There was no denying the sexual attraction, that was for sure. He could hardly remember his own name, watching Josie perform her little act. He generally preferred women in satin and lace, not latex and metal, but on Josie the look was wholly, undeniably *hot*.

"I'll have to handcuff you tonight, Slave."

She bent over him, her corseted cleavage making a lovely picture only inches from his nose, slipped a metal cuff around his wrist, then pulled both his hands behind the chair, where she cuffed them together. Trent heard the click of the locking mechanism and wasn't sure whether to be turned on or worried. Being totally at Josie's mercy couldn't be the smartest position he'd ever put himself in.

Trent stared at the circle of people watching him. There were seven couples present, of varying ages and degrees of weirdness. Poor saps. This is what happened when people got married and then got bored with each other. They had to start taking classes on how to tie each other up and give spankings.

If Trent was foolish enough to buy into the kind of mumbo jumbo taught at the Lovers for Life Center, he'd be living in the 'burbs, driving his two-point-five kids around in a minivan and dressing up as a Viking on Saturday nights to revitalize his dull married sex life.

Just the thought of it made him yawn. Contrary to popular belief, he'd had a few longish relationships, and after the initial new-person thrill wore off, they'd been about as exciting as plain white bread. That was why he preferred the one-week variety.

Okay, that and the fact that he refused to end up like his father. After a passionless twenty-five-year marriage to Trent's mother, the widower Tony O'Reilly had spent the past few years making a complete ass of himself. Once he'd recovered from his wife's death to cancer seven years ago, he'd run around like a horny teenager, getting it on with every sweet young thing in a skirt.

Trent figured the best way to avoid a passionless marriage was to cut things off before they had the opportunity to get boring. So Josie could instruct him as much as she wanted to about deep emotional commitments and how to give a woman toe-curling oral sex. He was way ahead of her, immune to the former and already an expert on the latter.

Josie cracked the whip again, this time managing not to hit him with it.

She turned to the class. "Some people find it arousing to be blindfolded. It increases the sense of powerlessness and the element of surprise. Others find the visual stimulation of the bondage scene to be more arousing."

To Trent she said, "Slave, you have no choice tonight. You don't deserve to look at me, so you'll be blindfolded."

"Yes, Mistress," he said, trying not to grin.

Trent wondered exactly how far she planned to take this little scenario. Not even her overly intellectual explanations of S&M could tame his raging libido—and he was enjoying this more than he cared to admit. Maybe it was time to spice things up even more.

As she approached him with a blindfold, he gave her his most earnest expression. "First, Mistress, may I lick your cleavage? Just once before you put the blindfold on?"

Josie stopped, her look of determination replaced by momentary shock. Then she recovered. "No, Slave, you may not."

"Your toes, then? I've always wanted to lick your toes."

Several class members snickered, and Josie's cheeks colored.

To Trent, she gave a warning glare and mouthed the words, "Quit it!" Then louder, for the class's benefit, "Tonight we'll learn the punishment for slaves who make unreasonable requests."

Trent smiled. "That's not what you said last night."

She wrapped the blindfold around his head and tied it in place. He then heard her footsteps heading in the direction of the table full of implements.

"What do you think, class? How should he be punished?"

A female voice said, "How about that thing with the spikes on it?"

"No, the muzzle," a male voice offered. "Make him wear the muzzle!"

Snickers and whispers traveled around the room as her footsteps approached him again.

"Slave, since you can't control your tongue, I'll have to control it for you."

All sort of lines about what he might do with his tongue came to mind, but before he could utter a word, Trent felt leather against his mouth and then straps being fastened behind his head.

"Mumph," he said, to test out exactly how much noise he could make with the thing on.

This was a first. He could honestly say he'd never been blindfolded and muzzled before.

Then he smelled the sweet citrus scent of Josie's perfume, and felt her breath against his cheek. "I'm sorry we had to resort to this, Slave. You'll respond to all further questions by nodding or shaking your head. Do you understand?"

Trent had a notion to lock his legs around his leather-clad captor and trap her there against him, but he thought of the whip she wielded like a drunken Zorro and decided against it. Instead he nodded, and she seemed to back away.

"One of the most fun aspects of bondage is the sensual teasing that can take place. When you have your spouse completely at your mercy, don't hesitate to drive him or her wild—that's the whole purpose! Seduction is all about the build-up, and your job as the dominant party is to leave your spouse begging and pleading for more."

Fine words from a woman who'd historically proven to be all build-up and no grand finale, Trent mused. She certainly could claim to be an expert on leaving men begging and pleading for more.

And then it struck him exactly how much trouble he might be in right now. Possibly major trouble. A whole heap of it.

"What do you think, Slave? Do you deserve to be tempted?"

Definitely major trouble.

Trent shook his head no.

"You're right, Slave. You don't. But for the sake of instruction, we're going to have a little fun without the blindfold."

He felt her undo the blindfold, and then he could see again. Josie stood in front of him, and as his gaze traveled up the length of her, she lifted one thigh-high boot to place the pointy toe right between his legs on the chair.

"Mumph," Trent said.

If he hadn't been muzzled, it would have come out as something slightly more explicit.

"I didn't give you permission to speak, Slave," Josie said with a playful glint in her eyes, "but I do give you permission to look now and to appreciate what you can't have.''

Apparently she'd gotten over her discomfort with the role of dominatrix and was starting to enjoy it. She nudged her toe forward until she bumped against his crotch. It was a gentle bump, but still, she was trespassing on sacred ground.

There would be time for retribution later. For now, Trent had little choice but to play along.

She leaned forward on her knee to offer him a prime view of her cleavage. Then her tongue flicked out and slowly traced her full lower lip.

''It's too bad you're so naughty, Slave, because I'm feeling very, *very* amorous,'' she whispered. ''Would you like to watch me touch myself?''

Trent suspected she was looking for an affirmative answer, and given the proximity of her boot, he nodded his head.

She smiled. ''Maybe later.''

And then she turned back to the class.

''Obedience, authoritarian roles, submission, level of punishment—these are all issues you'll have to work out between yourselves as a couple,'' Josie said, using her teacher voice again. ''I encourage you to come up and try out the various devices on the table, and there are also books and videos in the lobby, available for purchase.''

''Where do we get this stuff?'' someone asked.

''In your class handouts I've included a list of local retailers who carry bondage equipment.''

Trent watched Josie's sweet ass as she walked away—and out the door!—while students continued to mill around.

Hey, what about Slave Boy here? Was she just going

to leave him like this while students milled about? Was he supposed to be the test dummy for the novice sadists in the class?

"Mumph!"

"Ms. Marcus?" someone standing nearby called out. "I think your assistant wants to say something."

Trent stared at the doorway and listened for the sound of those spiked heels to return. Minutes ticked by, and his nose began to itch. Then a spot under the muzzle began to itch, too. He moved his jaw in a failed attempt to ease the itching.

If he'd come here looking for a renewed sense of resolve to keep on tormenting Josie, he'd certainly found it, and then some.

When the entire room had emptied, Trent sat wondering exactly how long she planned to leave him here. The contrast between leather-clad Josie and business Josie was striking. It surprised him to realize that he preferred the latter—though he had some ideas of what he might do with leather-clad Josie if she gave him half a chance.

Trent watched fifteen minutes tick by on the wall clock before Josie returned to the room. He'd expected her to have changed back into her business clothes, but she was still wearing the dominatrix getup. She carried a garment bag with what he assumed were her other clothes in it.

When she closed and locked the door behind her, his interest was piqued. The view of her backside, perfectly rounded and full in all the right places, designed for a man to grab on to during sex, didn't hurt.

She crossed the room and leaned over him again to remove the muzzle. But this time, her proximity and the lush upper halves of her breasts exposed by the corset, combined with the conveniently empty room, gave Trent an instant erection. Sex for him definitely wasn't a spectator sport. But given half a chance, he'd love to prop Josie up on that fold-out table full of bondage equipment and drive his cock into her until they were both gasping and sweating.

Whoa. Now that was exactly the kind of thinking that was going to ruin his plan. He was supposed to be exacting revenge on Josie, pleasure for pleasure, until she understood with painful certainty what it felt like to be left wanting more. Instead, he was spending way too much time thinking about what it would feel like to share with her a night of toe-curling orgasms.

"I guess you think that was funny, leaving me here bound and muzzled."

"It was necessary," she said, but a little smile revealed her true feelings.

"I had no idea you could be so kinky. Do you use those things with your boyfriends?" he asked, nodding to the muzzle.

Josie's smile transformed into a wicked grin. "Only when they need to be taught a lesson."

"And do I need to be taught a lesson?"

"You did hire me to do precisely that."

"I didn't agree to being bound and left alone when I'm supposed to be getting back to work."

Josie slid one corset strap off her shoulder, and Trent forgot what he'd just been protesting.

"So what's my lesson?"

"The importance of anticipation." She slid the other strap down, then began to unfasten the hooks on the front of the corset as she held her gaze level on him.

"Care to explain?" Trent said, pretending not to be absolutely riveted by her l...le show.

"Sometimes, what matters most about a satisfying sexual experience is the buildup. Not just the buildup of foreplay, but the buildup created by days or weeks of anticipation."

"You mean, playing the tease."

There was no mistaking the way her cheeks colored. But she didn't falter.

"No, because there's a real payoff at the end. There's a promise of good things to come."

She had reached the middle eye hooks and the corset was gaping open in the front, but not quite enough to reveal her breasts.

"So, what? You're going to get naked in front of me?"

"I'd call it a striptease, except I don't have any music."

She reached the last hook on the corset. Slowly she let it open and fall to her feet. Her brown nipples formed tight peaks, pulling her breasts taut. Trent almost couldn't look away, but somehow he managed to let his gaze travel down to her skintight black miniskirt, her thigh-high boots.

"Come over and sit on my lap and I'll give you your own little lesson about anticipation," he said, his voice sounding more strained than he'd hoped.

"No touching today—just looking. Next time, we touch."

She reached behind and unzipped her skirt, then pushed it over her hips and down her thighs. She was wearing a sheer little black lace thong for underwear. Beads of sweat broke out on the back of his neck.

"This is completely unfair. I ought to fire you."

"Do you feel a strong sense of anticipation?"

"I'm feeling a strong sense of anticipation to turn

you over my knee and spank you with one of those paddle things over there on the table," Trent lied.

His brain might have been resisting, but his body was riveted by her lesson like a straight-A student.

"So you *do* like it rough."

She placed her foot between his thighs on the chair again, this time to remove her boot. The view between her legs was almost more than Trent could take.

"No, I occasionally like it fast and hard, sometimes slow and easy, always hot and sweaty. But not rough."

She made no comment as she finished unlacing one boot and began working on the other. When that boot was unlaced, she tugged each one off and tossed them aside. In nothing but her thong panties, she stood right between Trent's legs, her own knees against the chair, her naked body close enough to touch.

"How's your feeling of anticipation now?" Her expression was vaguely amused, her tone teasing.

This was pure, uncensored Josie. She hadn't changed a bit in the years they'd been apart. And if Trent weren't so tense with pent-up sexual energy, he might have produced a witty comeback.

Instead he looked up at her and forced a smile. "I think you'd better get dressed and go have someone else take these handcuffs off of me. Then make sure you're nowhere to be seen when I leave the building, because otherwise—"

"And miss all the fun? No way."

She strolled over to the garment bag, grabbed it off a chair, then strolled back just as casually. As if she didn't have a clue what her naked body was doing to him physically. She was a good actress.

Trent watched in frustrated silence as she got dressed

in her work clothes. When she was finished, she turned to him and smiled.

"Anticipation—see how much fun it can be?"

Right. Fun. Trent and his rock-hard, no-hope-of-relief erection were having the time of their lives.

AFTER HER SLIGHTLY humiliating stint as a dominatrix, Josie spent the next week strategizing. She understood that it would take careful planning and calculated action to get Trent into bed, and she fully intended to achieve her goal. She'd rehearsed the necessary steps in her head a hundred times, and tonight she would begin to execute her new-and-improved seduction plan. If throwing herself at him wouldn't work, then she was just as capable of a covert operation.

Tonight's lesson on the anatomy of female arousal might have seemed on the surface to be fairly straightforward, even a bit simplistic for a guy who'd been around the block as many times as Trent had, but it was just one integral part of Josie's master plan.

Step One: build self-confidence in his sexual expertise by presenting him with an easy topic. Step Two: get him thinking in vivid detail about sex. Step Three: tempt him with a hands-on lesson. Step Four: get naked. And considering what a lather she'd left him in during her stint as a dominatrix, the rest would take care of itself.

However, if she'd miscalculated—if Trent hadn't gotten as worked up as she'd suspected during her strip-tease—there was always Plan B, in which Josie would resort to more aggressive tactics.

Okay, so Plan B wasn't as well thought out as Plan A. In fact, she couldn't be sure what her more aggressive tactics would be until the situation arose—or failed to *arise*. Josie winced at her own pun and decided to put the necessity for a Plan B out of her head. Positive thinking was mandatory for success, after all.

She surveyed her modest but comfy living room, wondering how it would look to Trent. Would he guess from her decorating taste that she was a sexually repressed nutcase? Would he suspect from the lack of family photos displayed anywhere that she had serious issues with her mother? Surely a guy like Trent wouldn't think that way. He'd probably just take one look at the lack of a recliner or big-screen TV and deem the place an uninteresting chick pad.

She was just letting the fear get to her. What she needed to do was visualize a successful seduction. As a therapist, she knew that visualization was a powerful tool for overcoming fears. And she'd already come up with the mental image she would use to calm her nerves when the time came—an image of her and Trent making passionate love on the floor of her living room.

She bent and plucked a piece of lint off the leopard-print throw rug—her one act of true decorative daring—and deposited it in the kitchen trash. There was no more obsessing or fidgeting left to do. If Trent didn't arrive soon, she was afraid she'd feel compelled to change her underwear and bra again, second-guessing her choice of a hot pink satin ensemble. Maybe he'd prefer something more subdued, or more innocent, or—

The doorbell rang and Josie hurried to the door and peered through the peephole. Trent stood in the hallway staring back at her, a bag of carry-out food in one hand. He looked downright edible in his black leather jacket and cream-colored turtleneck, and Josie decided she'd definitely ordered the wrong thing for dinner when she'd specified Kung Pao Chicken.

She reached for the doorknob and a sense of déjà vu came over her. Three years ago he'd shown up at her old apartment, just like this, wearing that same leather jacket. His arrival had been unannounced, but she'd known exactly what he wanted—an explanation for her inexcusable behavior at the beach. That night, though, she'd never answered the door.

She felt a great sense of shame at her cowardice. But no more. Tonight was the night she'd overcome her cowardly ways with Trent. Tonight was the night she'd face her fear and conquer it for good.

This time, she did open the door. "Come on in." Josie stepped aside and tried to appear casual, nothing like a woman who moments ago had been obsessing over her choice of coordinating bra and panties.

"Thanks for agreeing to have the lesson here at your place tonight. I don't know what to do about my dad."

"He must be lonely," Josie offered. Trent had called earlier to change the location of tonight's lesson from his apartment to hers, explaining that his father had practically taken up residence at his place after returning recently from a boating trip.

Trent shook his head. "He's never acted so strange before. I mean, he always drops by unannounced when he comes back to the city, but I'm starting to feel like I should be charging him rent."

"You're a good son to put up with him like that."

He shrugged. "How about we forget dear old dad and talk about something more interesting?"

Josie picked up her lesson materials from the nearby hallway table. Out of the folder she pulled an enlarged textbook-style diagram of a woman's body and spread it on the coffee table, setting in motion Plan A.

"Tonight's lesson," she said, "is on the anatomy of

female arousal. Why don't you study this while I get
our drinks?''

She held out a hand for the bag of carry-out and he
gave it to her. As he eyed the paper on the coffee table,
he sat on the sofa. Josie watched him from the corner
of her eye, curious to see what his reaction to the subject
would be.

''What can I get for you?''

''Got any beer?''

''Sure.'' Josie felt her cheeks burn, and she ducked
her head into the fridge to retrieve their drinks.

She hadn't anticipated how much their history could
come back to haunt her. The mention of beer immediately brought to mind sophomore year in high school,
when she and her best friend Amanda had gotten hold
of a couple of beers at a school football game and drank
them in the girls' bathroom. It had been Josie's first
taste of alcohol—and her first time kissing Trent, when
she'd met up with him later at halftime and they'd
slipped away together under the bleachers. Even then
the heat between them had been scorching, and Josie
had, like always, run away.

It was a wonder he'd even consider turning to her for
help with his sexual problems, with the way she'd
treated him back then.

She got out plates and forks and arranged their dinner
on trays so they could eat in the living room. She carried the trays in and placed one on each side of the
naked woman diagram.

''I hope you don't mind if I chow down before we
get started. I'm starved. Dad ate all the food in the
house.'' He stabbed a fork into his fried rice and started
eating.

"Sounds like he might be depressed. Is he dating anyone?"

"He was, but they broke up a few months back. I don't think that's the problem," he said between mouthfuls. "He wasn't serious about her at all—just another one of his midlife-crisis girls."

Josie frowned at her dinner, then took a bite. They small-talked their way through the rest of dinner, managing to avoid—much to Josie's relief—any discussion of the past. When they finished eating, Trent insisted on cleaning up before they started the lesson.

After he finished banging around in the kitchen, Trent came back into the living room, leaned over the coffee table and peered at the diagram. "What, exactly, am I supposed to learn from that picture?"

"It's a visual tool. Tonight you'll learn all about how to physically arouse a woman."

"I had a sex-ed class in junior high, and lots of hands-on experience since then. I think I can find the clitoris."

Oh, yes, he most certainly could. Josie blushed. "Trust me, this will be a far different lesson from any you had in school. And there's more to learn about the subject than the location of the clitoris."

Josie adjusted her sitting position on the floor and tried to ignore her growing sense of discomfort. Having Trent in her living room was sort of like having invited a lion from the zoo over for coffee. He seemed very large, very dangerous, and very out of place.

Josie fiddled with the charm bracelet on her left wrist, suddenly aware that this was the first time she'd had a man inside her new apartment. It was the first time a man had sat there on her celery-colored couch with its big comfy throw pillows.

Boy, did she ever need to get a life.

No time to fret now, though. She had a lesson to teach. "Take a good look at the picture and show me where a woman's major erogenous zones are located."

His eyebrows shot up and he smiled slyly. "I thought I showed you those last week."

He was clearly trying to rile her, and she wasn't going to fall for it. "For the sake of today's discussion, just point them out again."

Trent shrugged and gave the diagram a cursory glance. He went to Josie, offered her his hand, then pulled her up off the floor.

"Let's see…" He reached out and touched her neck, sending a wave of chills through her. "Here." He lowered his fingertips to her breast and brushed over one nipple lightly. "And here."

Oh, how her whole body begged for more of his touch. And then his hand dipped lower, going for the next danger—er, erogenous—zone.

Plan A was progressing even more smoothly than she'd anticipated. The way things were going, there definitely wouldn't be any need for a Plan B.

Trent's hand paused a few inches below Josie's belly button. "Ah, you meant, show you on the *diagram,* didn't you?"

"This way is fine, too," she assured him, trying her best not to sound too eager.

His trademark devil's grin appeared. "Oh, yeah?" His hand dipped lower. "And here, I've heard, there's another one."

Josie gasped at the exquisite sensation of his feather touch between her legs.

"Th-that's correct."

He removed his hand, and Josie willed herself not to grab it and press it right back where it belonged.

"So, do I pass the quiz?"

"You covered all the bases, but we'll be delving deeper than just the traditional erogenous zones."

"You mean, there are others I don't know about?"

"It could be said that the skin itself is a sex organ, and that's especially true for women. Where men are aroused primarily through stimulation to the sex organs, women can be aroused by stimulation to almost any area of the body, under the right circumstances."

Trent's eyebrows perked up. "Interesting."

"We'll be doing some hands-on…lab work, I guess you could call it."

"We learn by doing, right?"

"It'll require me to get undressed."

"Will this be part of that skills assessment I haven't taken yet?"

Josie pursed her lips, pretending to weigh the matter seriously. It wouldn't do for Trent to suspect she was determined to get that *skills assessment* from him if she had to tie him down and take it.

"Only if you're ready for it," she lied.

Trent crossed his arms over his chest, revealing pectoral muscles that bulged under his cotton shirt. "I've got to admit, I wasn't completely honest the other night when I said I wanted to take things slowly between us."

Oh, goody. Josie mentally rubbed her palms together. "What were your reservations, then?" she asked in as neutral a tone as she could muster.

He stared down at his black leather work boots. "To be honest, I'm kind of worried about my ability to, uh…perform with you."

Josie blinked. Never had she imagined perpetually

confident, ever-smirking Trent O'Reilly standing in front of her looking like such an uncertain little boy. Her heart warmed to his embarrassment. Of course, it was natural that he'd feel reservations about having sex with her, after admitting that he had trouble pleasing women in bed. He knew she'd be hyperalert to the issue. And she was a fool for not having anticipated this problem.

"There is absolutely nothing for you to be ashamed of. It takes real courage to admit you have this kind of problem and then go about trying to solve it the way you have."

He looked up at her and his expression brightened. "Really?"

"Really."

He frowned again. "I'm still not sure I'll be able to perform to the best of my ability. I mean, with it being a test and all."

Josie decided it was time to take action, before Trent completely lost his nerve. What he needed was a little enticement. She began to unbutton her top.

A surge of fear welled up in her chest. *Visualize, Josie. Visualize.* She automatically conjured up her sex-on-the-floor image and, like magic, the fear receded.

"Don't think of it as a test, because it's not. There is no passing or failing."

His gaze fell to her chest. He watched as she slipped the silky blue fabric over her shoulders, then let the top fall to the floor. Lust darkened his gaze, and panic seized Josie. Here she was again, so close, and yet still so ready to run away.

She willed herself to remain planted in that spot, to keep her eyes on the prize. She was only a few pieces of fabric away from reawakening her sex life, and she wasn't going to back down now. This was what she wanted. Yes, it definitely was.

And besides, she didn't have to fear sex with Trent being too overwhelming—or too anything. He was here for her help. He was nothing more than a delicious-looking sexual dud, and it was her job to train him.

"I'm willing to give it my best shot," he said, still focused on her hot-pink bra.

She'd made the right choice of undergarments, after all, it seemed.

"Good, then let's get back to our lesson." She went to Trent and took his hand, then led him to her bedroom, where the lights were already dimmed in preparation for the lesson. As she sat on the edge of her bed she explained, "I'd like us to spend some time exploring the many ways to physically arouse a woman."

Not that Josie needed arousing. She only needed to be in the same room with Trent for her panties to get wet. But what the heck, she could endure a little over-stimulation for the sake of Trent's education.

She just needed a mantra to keep herself in control. *Remember, he's a dud. He's a sexual dud.*

"I'm at your command," Trent said, his gaze moving from her to the new surroundings.

She watched him as he took in the small bedroom decorated in what Josie liked to think of as shabby chic. Shabby, because she spent a lot of her free time rummaging through second-hand stores and estate sales. She'd found her ornate mahogany bed and matching dresser at an estate sale in Boston, and with a little work she'd turned it into a beautiful set again, but it still bore the wear of a hundred years of use. The room was decorated in whites and reds, with lots of striped fabrics contrasting with red rose prints.

What Trent probably saw was a frilly, girly haven.

A small Victorian tassel lamp lit the room, casting shadows over the familiar planes of Trent's face. He had a five o'clock shadow, barely noticeable, but just enough to remind Josie that he was no longer the cute boy from down the block. He was a grown man, with adult needs that her body ached to fulfill.

"So this is your learning laboratory?" he asked.

Josie smiled. "I have to admit, there hasn't been much learning going on in here so far. But we'll fix that."

She extended her hand and he took it, then allowed her to pull him onto the bed beside her.

"Your task," she said, "is to arouse me without touching any of those spots you pointed out earlier as being erogenous zones."

He narrowed his eyes. "Oohh, you tricked me."

"I think you're up for the challenge."

"I'm up for it, all right." He leaned over her then and kissed her, delving in tentatively.

Josie welcomed his tongue, welcomed the warmth and the hunger. And then he pulled back.

"I can touch you here?" He trailed his fingers lightly along her rib cage, under the curve of her breast, then slowly down the center of her belly as she leaned back on her elbows. He stopped at her belly button and circled.

"Mmm-hmm."

"By touch, I'm assuming you mean with my hands *or* my mouth, right?"

Oh, yes. She nodded, closing her eyes to savor the

sensation of his fingers gliding over her flesh. And then his lips touched her belly and she squirmed with delight.

Okay, so she wasn't the most challenging woman to arouse. Trent could simply breathe in her direction and she'd get all worked up. But he didn't have to know that.

He unfastened her jeans and pulled them down her hips, then off her legs. He climbed back onto the bed and hovered over her, his delicious heat warming her bare flesh. And then he dipped his head to her stomach again.

"How's this?" he asked between butterfly kisses around her belly button.

Josie sank back on the bed and stretched her arms over her head. "I think you're getting the idea," she said, her voice amazingly controlled.

His tongue dipped into her navel, and she squirmed at the tickling sensation. He moved lower, his fingers and lips tickling and tasting her hip, her outer thigh, her inner thigh… Oh, if he would only move a few inches to the left, she'd be in heaven. But he was carefully following her rules, behaving like an obedient student. Damn her stupid rules.

Josie gasped as he teased the delicate skin of her inner thigh with his lips and traced the curve of her buttocks with his fingertips. He moved lower yet again, this time to the backs of her knees, her calves, her ankles. Josie's skin was dotted with gooseflesh, her breathing shallow, her thoughts ajumble.

Out of nowhere a coherent thought appeared. She found herself wishing she and Trent were more than just student and teacher. Having him here in her bedroom with her felt…right. There was no other way to describe it. Her usual fear of Trent's sexual power over her had disappeared, to be replaced by this strange feeling of rightness.

But no, that had to be desperation clouding her common sense. As soon as she got him to make love to her, surely she'd get her head on straight.

Trent's lips, working magic on her inner thigh, forced all thoughts from her mind again.

And then, suddenly, the delicious sensations stopped. Josie's eyes popped open. Her view of the ceiling turned into a view of Trent, kneeling over her, wearing a pained expression. Did her feet smell bad? Had she forgotten to shave her legs?

"I know I said I could do this..." Trent began, "but..."

Oh, no, not again. Josie pushed herself up onto her elbows.

"It's completely natural for you to feel some reservations. I'm sorry, I've given you performance anxiety by presenting this as a skills assessment."

He raked his fingers through his hair and exhaled. "I guess I do feel a little like I always did before a big exam in school."

Damn it, why hadn't she thought of this possibility? She'd been so blinded by her desire to get laid, she'd gotten careless in her planning. Okay, okay, all wasn't lost yet.

"You want to become an expert lover, right?"

"I don't know. Maybe this is all a big mistake, these sex lessons." He got up from the bed, and Josie's body turned cold.

She suddenly felt naked and ridiculous. "It isn't a mistake for you to realize you have a problem and try to fix it."

"I'm sorry I've wasted your time like this," he said. "But I think we'd better stop right now, before we do something we'll both regret."

Josie shot up to a sitting position, her desire-addled brain trying to process how the evening had gone so quickly awry. She could have kicked herself for not developing a Plan B ahead of time. Now that she was here, in the heat of the moment, no brilliant ideas were popping into her head.

Trent was straightening his shirt, backing up toward the door…retreating. Mere seconds ago their little sex lesson had been progressing quite well, and now he was leaving. She'd scared him away.

This was just her luck. Even after throwing herself at a guy twice—a guy who was basically paying her for sex—Josie still couldn't manage to get herself laid.

She smiled with as much dignity as she could muster. "I'm beginning to think you don't approve of my teaching methods."

"No, it's not that. It's just me. I'm afraid—" Trent wore such a puppy-dog expression, Josie couldn't help but let some of her frustration melt away.

"Say no more. Next lesson I'll be sure to, um, adjust my lesson plan to fit your needs."

Yeah, she'd adjust her lesson, all right—adjust it to include a sturdy pair of handcuffs to keep Trent right where she wanted him.

TRENT GAZED UP at the building Extreme Sports had occupied ever since he'd taken over the business from his father seven years ago. He'd promptly turned the store from a traditional sporting goods shop into a specialty retailer catering to extreme athletes. It carried everything from mountain climbing equipment to body surfing suits.

The square white stucco structure lacked any real aesthetic appeal, but it still looked like home to Trent. He'd come to the store as a kid, played in the stockroom, pretended to help his father with the cash register. Not even the store's hip young makeover could make him forget the old leathery smell of his father's store, or the way his dad had always let him play catch indoors— something strictly forbidden at home.

He tried to imagine driving by in a few months to find the building gone, the space occupied by a monolithic bookstore. His gut twisted into a knot. That wasn't what he wanted, was it? Or was he letting sentimentality get in the way of good business sense? The money MegaBooks was offering would be enough to not only secure his retirement income, but also provide him with more than enough capital to get his outdoor adventure business firmly established in Tahoe.

And then there was the Lovers for Life Center. Rafaela and Josie could always lease a building elsewhere and move the business. But as rocky as their finances seemed to be, having to relocate now would surely drive them into bankruptcy. Even if they could survive a move, Trent wasn't even sure they could find the right kind of business space in a desirable location without spending months and months looking for it.

Trent shook his head and walked the short distance to his car as he dug in his pocket for the keys. He was leaving Max to close the store tonight, so he could take the car to the body shop and leave it there for repair.

When he reached the Porsche, parallel parked on the curb, he bent to take another look at the dent on the bumper. It was a semipermanent reminder that Josie had slammed back into his life. Damn that woman and her lousy driving skills. She was parked behind him again, her beat-up old Saab with its ridiculous headlight wipers—who needed automatic wipers for their headlights in California?—sitting there seeming to mock him.

"If there's another dent, I didn't do it." It was Josie's voice, right behind him.

Trent turned to find her standing on the sidewalk, looking particularly pretty in the golden sunset light that poured in from the west end of the street. Streaks of silver-blond in her hair caught the evening sun, and her skin had the sort of glow he imagined most women applied lots of lotions and powders to achieve. Josie had always possessed that eye-catching glow. It was one of the qualities that made Trent find it nearly impossible not to stare at her.

"You sound a little defensive. Maybe I should be looking for more damage?"

"That dent was a freak accident. I don't make a habit of hitting cars."

Trent shifted his gaze to her dent-riddled junker.

"Then they must run into you. Out of nowhere. Constantly. Right?"

She repressed a smile. "Absolutely."

"Liar."

Josie's expression sobered. "I was hoping to catch you. About the other night…"

Trent willed himself to keep a straight face. "I'm sorry I've been disrupting the course of your lessons."

"Do you still want to continue them?"

"Definitely. And I promise, next time I'll be ready to do whatever you want."

She smiled. "Good. There's something else I'd like to discuss. I'm hoping to arrange a time when we could talk business, if you don't mind."

"What sort of business?"

"It's about the center. I need a little advice from someone who knows how to run a business successfully."

The idea of spending an evening not focused on sex with Josie—or the avoidance of it—struck Trent with unexpected appeal. He hadn't realized until that moment how much he wanted to just sit down and talk to her.

"I don't know how much help I can be, but I'd be happy to try. I have to take my car to the body shop right now. Want to meet up afterward?"

She winced. "I'm sorry I don't have the cash to pay for the damage."

"Hey, that's part of our deal, remember? I said I'd forgive the rent debt and the car damage cost."

"Still, I feel bad about it. Won't you need a ride after you drop off your car?"

"I was going to walk, but yeah, I could use a ride."

He eyed Josie's dent mobile. "I'm not sure I have the stomach to ride with you, though."

She rolled her eyes. "I think you'll survive."

On the way to the body shop, Josie followed in her clunker. Trent tried to keep his mind on driving, but every glance at Josie in the rearview mirror brought his thoughts back to their last lesson five nights ago. Five long, agonizing nights ago.

From her demeanor, Trent figured Josie hadn't suspected that he'd lied about his reason for not wanting to have sex. But even he didn't want to consider the real reason. It certainly wasn't performance anxiety, yet it wasn't simply the desire to get even with her, either.

As much as he hated to admit it, he'd felt some pretty strong emotions during their last lesson. Being in Josie's apartment, sharing Chinese take-out, he'd found himself wishing he'd been there on a regular date; imagining them as a real couple; wanting them to go to bed together in that overly romantic, flowery bedroom of hers and wake up the next morning together.

It was just all the sexual deprivation going to his head. Ever since he'd managed to put the brakes on having sex with her yet again, he'd slept like hell. His dreams consisted of torturous images of Josie, tormenting him, teasing him, driving him to the edge of insanity. And his waking thoughts were no more comforting. It took all his willpower not to slip into the bathroom and relieve himself of what seemed like one long, endless hard-on.

But all he needed to do to summon his strength again was to remember his goal—revenge. He needed only to close his eyes and picture Ocean Beach, recall the sight of Josie's taillights as she'd pulled away, relive the feeling of utter betrayal that wrenched his gut that night, and he was fortified for as long as it would take.

They arrived at the body shop on Geary Street and Trent parked his car and went inside to drop off the keys. When he came back out, he found Josie standing next to the Porsche, waiting for him.

"Someone will come out in a minute to take a look at the damage, and then we can go."

"No hurry," she said, turning her attention to the Porsche. "This is a beautiful car."

"Thanks."

She cast a sideways glance at him. "You do know what sports cars represent for the male psyche, don't you?"

Trent stuck his hands into his back pockets. "Let me guess. It means I'm overcompensating for a small penis and an even smaller sense of self-esteem?"

She grinned. "Not exactly. For you, I'm guessing it's a way of holding on to a sense of freedom and youth. But there is that manhood issue."

"I'm dying to hear this."

"Men who drive sports cars tend to be a little insecure about their male identity."

"I'm plenty secure. And I didn't ask you to psychoanalyze me, all right?"

"I can understand why you'd be uncomfortable with that," she said in a tone that suggested she was enjoying ribbing him.

What he wanted to do was to pull her into a dark corner at that moment and kiss her senseless, but that would probably suggest something about his male identity, too.

"I'm not uncomfortable with it. I just don't need it."

Out of the corner of his eye he caught her smiling to herself. "Sure, okay."

A man in blue coveralls appeared with a clipboard in his hand to inspect the car damage. Trent showed him the dent and watched as the man squatted to take a closer look at the damage. He began making notes on the clipboard, and when he finished, he stood and stuck his ink pen in a chest pocket.

"It'll be about two thousand to do the repairs. We'll have to replace the bumper panel and paint the new body piece."

Trent shrugged. No one ever said owning a Porsche was cheap—thank God for insurance. "Sounds fine."

Beside him, Josie looked stricken.

"Can you pick it up in five days?"

He had an old sport utility vehicle he drove on his trips to the mountains, so lack of transportation wasn't an issue. "No problem." Trent handed over the keys and took the estimate sheet the mechanic offered him.

He and Josie walked to her car, and he remembered as he got in that the last time he'd ridden with her had been three years ago...

A sick feeling invaded his stomach. He willed the negative memory away. Right now, it was the last thing he wanted to think about.

When Josie got into the driver's seat, Trent asked, "So, do you want to brief me on this business issue you need to discuss?"

She grinned sheepishly as she started the car. "I'm not very good at talking and driving at the same time."

"Oh, right." He appreciated her honesty.

"Where do you want to go?"

"Someplace that serves food. I'm starved."

Josie pulled out into traffic without incident and navigated her way eight or ten blocks down to an empty parking spot.

"There's a place on this block called El Corazon Café that has great salsa. Sound okay?" she asked as they got out of the car.

"Sounds perfect."

They walked toward the restaurant with a crisp ocean breeze at their backs, and Trent tried not to notice how it made Josie's suit form to every tempting line of her body. He walked faster to rid himself of the view, but that only made her mad.

"Hey, wait up!" she called as she hurried behind him.

"Sorry, forgot my manners."

"Are you embarrassed to be seen with me?"

Trent laughed. "Hardly. I was just trying to avoid staring at your ass, if you want to know the truth."

"Oh." She stopped walking, and Trent realized they'd made it to the restaurant.

With its brightly colored walls painted with hearts and cacti and other less recognizable objects, and its wild, funky tables and chairs, the restaurant fit in quite well with this business district. Trent could have done without the polka-dot chairs, but he was hungry enough to ignore them.

They placed their orders at the counter, then found a table near the front window. Since it was nearly eight o'clock the big dinner crowd was gone and they had a bit of privacy.

Josie cut right to the point. "You're aware of the Lovers for Life Center's financial difficulties."

Trent nodded, adjusting his feet under the table. He accidentally bumped her leg and the sudden contact put his nerves on alert. Damn it, how did she do that to

him? The woman had an uncanny knack for turning
him on.

"I'm afraid it's even worse than a few late rent payments," she said.

"What else are you behind on?"

Josie's gaze dropped to her hands as she fiddled with
a napkin. "I have a list of the late bills in my office,
but I can't remember off hand."

"Are you even turning a profit right now?"

Josie shook her head. "Hardly. We're losing
money."

Trent hadn't realized the extent of the center's trou-
bles, and now he felt a tiny pang of guilt for putting
Josie in such a compromising position by asking her for
private sex lessons. He'd held on to the far-fetched belief, in the back of his head, that she could have af-
forded to pay the rent if she'd really wanted to, that
she'd just accepted the offer in the spirit of their long-
standing sexual rivalry.

"Why come to me?"

Josie regarded him levelly, making a great internal
effort, he guessed, to separate her current needs from
what happened between them five nights ago. Trent
wasn't sure he could accomplish that feat himself.

He'd spent every day since the last lesson trying to
summon up the willpower to resist Josie during the next
one. If he gave in to her, his revenge plan would be
ruined. And spending time around Josie only made him
like her more, thus weakening his defenses. With her
popping back into his life today—two days early—
she'd thrown off his plan.

"You run a successful business. I was hoping you
might help me figure out if I have a chance of saving

the center, and how to go about bringing in more money.''

''I know nothing about operating a school.''

She nodded. ''True, but I need a fresh perspective on the problems I'm dealing with. Maybe I could run some ideas by you and you could give me your reactions.''

''Sure.''

The waiter delivered their dinners, and the scent of fresh cilantro reminded Trent that he was hungry. They both dove into their burritos and ate in silence for a few minutes.

Trent mulled over the possible business problems the Lovers for Life Center faced. How ''in demand'' could sex classes be? There must have been enough of a need for the business to keep running for more than twenty years.

''How's enrollment at the center?'' he asked between bites.

''Down since I took over. My mother was the heart of the place, and it's not the same without her.''

''Have your customers said as much?''

''We've had quite a few complaints about her absence.''

Trent could imagine the hole Rafaela's departure would leave. She had a commanding presence, and she was a tireless self-promoter, often appearing on local television shows and in newspaper interviews talking about sex.

''What other changes have occurred since she left?''

''I've had to stop inviting a lot of our guest speakers. They were just too expensive, but they brought in nonregular attendees of the seminars. It was a big profit-maker.''

Trent polished off the last bite of his burrito and

turned his attention to the chips and salsa. "Have you tried this stuff?"

Josie nodded. "It's the best. They make it fresh every morning."

She took a chip and dipped it, then brought it to her lips. Trent never would have labeled eating a corn chip an erotic act, but watching her do it—yow. He stared, mesmerized, as she tasted the salsa, smiled, closed her eyes and moaned with pleasure.

When she finished the chip she licked a dab of salsa from her finger, and Trent felt beads of sweat break out on his forehead. He wanted her now just as badly as he always had. What disconcerted him was that the desire only seemed to grow more intense each time they were together. It had to be all the teasing—that was it.

"Mmm, that's the best salsa in the city."

Only then did she seem to notice him staring, and she averted her gaze. When she looked at him again, he'd wiped away the sweat and gathered his composure. "Spicy food always makes me hot."

She smiled. "Yeah, me, too."

Okay, time to focus on something nice and safe. "What are your ideas to increase business?"

She took a deep breath and began. "One of our strengths is our repeat business, but frankly, there are only so many sex workshop topics I can offer. I mean, things get repetitive after a while."

"Which is fine for one-time or infrequent attendees."

"Right." Her brow creased, and Trent had to resist the urge to reach out and run his fingers along her temples to release some of her stress.

But touching her once would be a mistake. Everything about her made him want to touch her, explore the planes and valleys of her body, find her secret places. Okay, so he'd already found some of those, but damn if he didn't want to get to know them even better.

"I need to find a way to provide new interests for repeat customers and potential repeat customers, and I have one idea."

"Which is?"

"It has to do with you, actually."

"Me?" Trent blinked. He absolutely was not going to teach a sex class, if that's what she had in mind.

"I saw a sign on the door of Extreme Sports the other day, and ever since then I've had this idea forming."

"Wilderness sex tours?" he joked.

"Well, not exactly, but…"

"Oh, no. Don't even think about it."

She winced at his reaction. "Just hear me out. Please?"

"I'm not taking a bunch of horny couples out to have sex in the wild."

"You're oversimplifying my idea. Let me finish."

He leaned back in his chair and crossed his arms over his chest, but said no more.

"A lot of men, apparently, including yourself, have these outdoorsy, wilderness sex fantasies. And a lot of couples seem to love having sex in places that they might get caught."

"By bears?"

"Well, I doubt that's what they have in mind, but I think any location outside their own homes provides a heightened sense of excitement for them."

"Uh-huh."

"I think I could draw in quite a few customers by offering romantic adventure retreat weekends."

"Retreat?"

"I would go along and offer workshops, and you could be there for the adventure and outdoors stuff."

"So what? I'd have to take them out and show them where the prime sex spots are in the woods?"

"Not at all. It would be pretty much like one of your regular tours. Except you might have to count on people sneaking off for a little hanky panky occasionally."

"I'm guessing these couples wouldn't want to rough it too much."

"Probably not."

Trent let the idea sink in. It wasn't a bad one, actually.

"There aren't any luxury hotels in the wilderness. No hot tubs, no room-service food to tank up on between rounds of wild sex."

"Do all your tours involve camping, or do you ever go to cabins?"

"We do have cabins sometimes, nothing fancy."

"I'm thinking that would be best. Cabins would provide privacy for those who need it."

Like us.

Whoa. Where had that thought come from? He hadn't even agreed to lead the tours and already he was having fantasies of getting Josie alone in the woods.

"I know a place out near Tahoe that would be great for what you have in mind. Beautiful scenery, easy hiking trails, nice cabins, and there are other facilities where you could lead your sex classes."

"We would need to work out the costs, how we'd split the expenses and profits."

"I usually lead more advanced tours than what you have in mind."

Josie frowned. "But couldn't you ease up a bit? Maybe offer a sort of beginners adventure weekend?"

An idea nagged at the back of Trent's brain. If they planned this right, it could work to his benefit, too. He'd been mulling over designing a tour for a less experienced crowd than the one he usually attracted. It would be a great way to increase business.

"Okay, let's do it," Trent said. "I'll give you the trip costs tomorrow so you can make up something to advertise to your customers."

Her face lit up. "Really? You'll do it?"

"For you, sure. I'll even provide all the gear. On one condition."

"Anything—you name it."

Trent blurted what he wanted before he had a chance to change his mind. "Go out mountain biking with me one day while we're there, just the two of us."

"But, why?"

Good question, and he didn't have an answer, so he made one up. "For old times' sake."

Josie gave him a speculative look. "But you'll actually expect me to ride a bike?"

"Yes. Will that be so awful?"

"Don't you remember that time I wrecked my pink Huffy into the Cirenzas's Volkswagen van?"

Trent smiled at the long-forgotten memory. "Oh, yeah, that was you, wasn't it? Even back then you were a bad driver."

"That was the last time I rode a bike."

Oh, boy, would he ever be in for an interesting weekend. He shrugged, still too enamored with the idea of having Josie around twenty-four hours a day to back down. "You know what they say about riding a bike."

Josie bit her lip, gave the matter some thought. "Okay, I'll do it. But don't expect me to survive."

"You'll be fine."

"I want to get this trip off the ground as soon as possible."

"Like when?"

"There's a long weekend at the end of this month," she said, her eyes full of hope that he'd okay the date.

Trent groaned. "I need more notice than that usually."

"But you don't have plans that weekend, do you?"

He rolled his eyes at his own lack of a spine. "No. I'll see what I can do."

"You're the best! I mean, this isn't going to save the center, but it's one step in the right direction. I feel like it's the first good idea I've had since I took over."

Trent nodded. "Why don't we continue our discussion of ways to improve business tomorrow, when I can give you the estimated trip costs?"

"That's perfect—we can meet in my office after classes are over. Thank you, thank you, thank you!" She stood, leaned over the tiny table, and kissed him. He could tell immediately by her chagrined expression that she'd acted on impulse.

It didn't matter, though. One warm simple kiss erased all his reservations. A long weekend in the woods with Josie? It sounded like heaven.

RAFAELA MARCUS watched through the airplane window as the San Francisco skyline came into view over the water. Her beautiful city, still here waiting for her. Prague had been interesting, but it couldn't compare to home.

She glanced at her watch and saw that the flight was arriving twenty minutes early. It might be the first time in her life she'd ever be early for anything. If only her darling Josephine were here to witness the event...

But no, if all had been going well here at home, Josephine should have been having herself a grand time this weekend with a certain gorgeous young landlord Rafaela knew was perfect for her daughter. She also knew Josephine was far too young and stubborn to understand her mother's wisdom, so subtle tactics had been required.

Josephine didn't need to know that Peter, Rafaela's "lover," was really just a close friend, and a gay one at that. At half her age, and as beautiful as he was, he might have made a fine playmate, but she'd outgrown such antics long ago, and she and Peter didn't share the slightest attraction for one another.

She gripped the arm of her seat as the plane touched down with a bump-bump-bump, then settled into a smooth path on the runway.

Nor did her daughter need to know that her mother's disappearance was more for Josephine's sake than anything else. The poor girl just didn't know how to have a good time, but Rafaela suspected Trent could teach her, if the two could only see their way past a few superficial differences.

She flipped through a mindless beauty magazine as other passengers filled the aisles and grabbed their bags. Once the plane had started to clear out, Rafaela stood and shrugged her carry-on over her shoulder, then exited the plane.

In the airport she headed straight for the nearest book stand to arm herself with a little reading material for the weekend ahead. Once she'd gotten her copy of the latest erotic thriller by her favorite author, she was ready to call a cab. She might be getting older, but she certainly wasn't dead yet.

First, though, she needed to find out where Josephine

was. She wasn't quite ready to let her daughter know she was home. There was detective work to be done. She needed to know exactly how far Trent and Josephine's relationship had progressed, and whether any further intervention would be required. Rafaela stopped at a pay phone, fed it some change, and dialed the number to the center. Knowing her workaholic daughter, she would be there now.

"Lovers for Life Center, may I help you?" Josephine answered after a few rings.

"Josephine, it's Mom. Just calling to say hi."

"Oh, hi, Mom. What's up?"

"Nothing important. I was hoping to find you'd gone out for the evening with a man instead of sitting in that office alone, working late."

A pause. "I'm not alone, actually."

"Oh?"

"I'm just talking to someone about the business."

"And whom would that be?"

Another pause. "Trent O'Reilly. He's helping me develop a plan to solve our financial problems."

Rafaela bit her tongue to avoid letting out a joyful whoop. If she overtly pushed her daughter, Josephine would dig in her heels and a month of progress would be lost.

"That's nice, darling," she finally said. "I hope there's not a problem with the rent."

Josephine made a little "ahem" sound. "Now that you mention it, there have been problems keeping up with the rent. I don't suppose you've gotten any of the money back from Peter?"

Rafaela winced. If there'd been a less drastic way of getting those two together, she would have used it. At least her plan seemed to be working. "No, I'm afraid not. He's having a terrible time selling his book," she lied.

In truth, she hadn't loaned a cent to Peter. The money she'd taken from the business account had simply been deposited into her savings account before she left the country. It had been the only way Rafaela could think of to ensure Josephine and Trent would have to work through a little adversity together.

"Is there anything you need, Mom? If not, I really shouldn't keep Trent waiting."

"Oh, no, by all means, I'll let you go." Rafaela paused, wishing she had the kind of relationship with her daughter in which they could truly share their secrets. Instead, Josephine always held her at arm's length, embarrassed by her mother's every move. She finally added, "Don't forget to have fun."

"Are you sure everything's okay? It sounds really noisy there."

"I just have the windows open, and there's a traffic jam on the street outside." A voice came over the airport intercom system calling for passenger so-and-so to report to gate something-or-other, and Rafaela quickly covered the phone.

"That sounded like a woman's voice."

"It's the television. Peter's watching for inspiration," she lied. Peter didn't even own a television.

"Oh. Well, bye, Mom. Talk to you later."

"Bye-bye."

Rafaela hung up the receiver and frowned. She'd have to lay low for the weekend and do a little investigating to see how Josephine and Trent's relationship had progressed. If the two young people hadn't at least become lovers by now, she'd be forced to resort to more drastic measures.

8

TRENT ENTERED his living room and smelled the distinct odor of hundred-dollar aftershave hanging in the air. Immediately his shoulders tensed and his stomach rolled over. His dad was here. Any night but tonight. Not tonight.

But the sound of a bad rendition of Tom Jones coming from the shower confirmed it; his dad had dropped in again.

Ever since Trent's mother had passed away, his father had drifted, pursuing his dream of traveling the world on his boat. But his heart had never really been in it. It was almost as if he missed his late wife, but Trent knew better than to believe that. His parents may have had a companionable relationship, but they'd seemed more like roommates than husband and wife. Trent had witnessed the petty bickering, the lack of passion—and recently the incessant skirt-chasing that proved his dad wasn't pining after his dead wife.

His father had returned last month from a long boat trip, and after one of those he always got antsy for a real house. He'd drop by unannounced to take a shower, cook a meal, or generally just to meddle in Trent's life.

These days Trent alternated between feelings of anger at his father for going through women faster than he could count—many of them young enough to be Trent's sisters—and feelings of pity for his lonely father.

He went into the kitchen to grab a beer, and by the time he'd downed half of it his dad was out of the bathroom, strolling through the apartment in a towel.

"Hey, son, you're home!" Tony said as he entered the kitchen and gave Trent a mock punch in the shoulder.

His father was a big man, still solid muscle even in his early fifties, with the dark tan of an avid sailor. He took pride in his appearance and even with salt-and-pepper hair, Tony O'Reilly could still manage to catch the attention of plenty of women when he entered a room.

"Hey, Dad. You could have called first. I've got plans in the apartment tonight."

His father pulled eggs and cheese from the fridge and started searching the cabinets for, Trent assumed, a pan. He finally found a skillet and fired up a burner. "Good to see you, too. Don't mind me—you won't even notice I'm here."

"I have *private* plans."

Trent had two brothers, Drew and Jake, who'd both moved to landlocked areas after finishing college. It made it much harder for their dad to make his infamous drop-in visits that way. While Trent appreciated having his father around, it was the drop-in, unexpected aspect of his visits that tended to cramp Trent's style. Denver was suddenly starting to sound like a nice place to live.

Anthony proceeded to make an omelet as Trent downed the rest of his beer. His father sang his rendition of Tom Jones's "Sex Bomb" while he cooked, totally off key and oblivious.

When he finished and sat down to eat, he took one look at Trent's face and laughed. "Don't worry, boy.

You got a lady coming over? I'll be out of your hair in a half hour, tops.''

He hadn't wanted to admit to his father that he had a relationship with anyone, since this invariably invited meddling. But a woman coming over was the one reason Tony would willingly vacate the premises, no questions asked. He'd never want to interrupt an evening with a lady.

When his father finally left, Trent scrambled to get rid of the funky smell in the apartment, dispose of empty pizza boxes, and straighten up enough so that Josie wouldn't think he was one of those guys who was helpless around the house without a woman. He didn't feel like examining why her opinion mattered so much, but he feared it had a lot to do with that fuzzy feeling in his gut that appeared every time he thought of Josie lately.

He was about as good at this revenge stuff as a love-sick puppy.

Josie arrived right on time, wearing a trench coat belted at the waist. Trent was just as aware as the next guy what women generally wore underneath trench coats when they showed up at a guy's door, and he wasn't sure whether to thank heaven or to run for the hills.

"Hey, come on in," Trent said, unable to tear his gaze away from her black pantyhose-clad calves that led up to…what? He was dying to know.

She entered, carrying a large black bag that she placed beside the couch. And when she noticed his curiosity she explained, "This lesson involves a few, um, props."

Interesting. Memories of Trent's short stint as Josie's

slave-boy assistant appeared, and he wondered if these would be props he recognized.

"Can I take your coat?"

She crossed her arms over her chest. "I'm a little chilly, actually. Maybe in a few more minutes."

"Suit yourself. Want anything to drink? I'm getting myself a beer."

"Don't bother," she said. "You won't be able to drink it."

Trent stopped in his tracks halfway to the kitchen, an image of himself in a dog muzzle flashing in his mind. "Because?"

Josie smiled a seductive smile and began to unbutton her coat. "Tonight's lesson is about the eroticism of control—or lack of it."

She opened the coat and shrugged it off her shoulders, revealing a black lace bustier of the sort he'd imagined naughty French maids wore. She had on matching black lace panties and a garter belt that held up sheer black hose.

"I don't guess I'll get to be the one in control."

She came toward him. "I think you have issues with letting go, so we're going to work on that tonight."

"Let me just say right now, no more whips or muzzles."

She stopped in front of him, only inches away, and motioned to a dining room chair. "Of course not. Now have a seat and we'll get started."

If he gave Josie control, his revenge plan would be out the window, but he couldn't summon the will to care. They'd both suffered enough, hadn't they?

Trent sat and she straddled his lap. The sudden intimate contact, the heat of her body against him, was nearly too much. He slid his hands around her waist and cupped her buttocks. His cock instantly grew hard.

She shook a finger at him. "No touching, not until I give you permission."

"But you get to touch me?"

"Mmm-hmm. Wherever I want."

Oh, yeah. Trent could dig this forceful side of Josie.

"All sexual relationships are a balance of enticement and satisfaction, temptation and release, control and abandonment—the ever-shifting power struggle between man and woman."

With that, she was up off his lap and rummaging in the mysterious black bag. She withdrew a familiar-looking pair of handcuffs and a red scarf.

"Is that what we've been doing all this time? Having a power struggle?"

"Maybe," she said.

"Excuse my language, but that's a load of psycho-babble crap."

Josie frowned at him. "This is all part of the lesson. You want my expertise, right?"

He nodded, more than ready to play along with her game, even if he did think she was full of it.

"Then don't ask questions, just do what I say. We can discuss the lessons learned at the end."

She tugged his arms down and behind the chair. He felt the handcuffs fasten around one of his wrists. Then she slipped the free end through one of chair slats and cuffed the other wrist.

"You're becoming quite the bondage expert."

She sighed theatrically. "All for the sake of your education."

Next came the scarf to cover his eyes.

"Is that really necessary?" he said as she secured the scarf.

"Absolutely. When vision is impaired, the other senses are heightened. And I told you not to ask questions."

"I thought all teachers liked curious stu—"

She cut him off with a soft, slow kiss. And then she was gone. A moment later music began to play on the stereo, a slow jazz tune, and he could hear the barely audible fall of her footsteps on the carpet as she returned to him.

And then she was unbuttoning his shirt, opening the fly of his jeans. Trent let out a soft groan when her hand brushed his erection through the fabric of his boxers.

Her breath tickled his neck and she whispered, "Do you like it when I touch you there?"

"Yes," he said, his voice strained. "I do."

She slid her hand down his thigh and back up, but avoided his groin and continued up his belly to his chest. Lightly she pinched one nipple, then the other. She pulled aside his shirt and her hair brushed against him as she tasted each nipple, then trailed kisses up his chest to his neck.

When her hand found his penis and began to massage softly, Trent gasped and let his head fall back.

"Would you like it if I touched you there with my mouth?"

He groaned. "Yes," he managed to say.

She had complete control over him, and not just physically. He couldn't think of a single reason why he'd ever wanted to seek revenge against her.

A moment later he felt her lips on the head of his penis, then her tongue, and he lost all sense of reason.

She took him into her mouth and began a rhythmic movement, her tongue teasing, coaxing him to release.

His wrists strained against the handcuffs, he so desperately wanted to take her and find release, but then she quickened her pace and he felt the great rush of his climax coming.

"Stop!" he gasped. When he came for the first time with Josie, it wouldn't be like that.

And then her mouth was gone. The ache of its absence consumed Trent, but he wanted her now. Not just her teasing.

She removed the blindfold and he blinked in the soft lamplight. She stood over him, watching him catch his breath.

"You liked that."

"Yeah," he croaked, still gasping.

"You'll need your sight for what happens next."

Trent smiled. "I can't wait."

"But you're not satisfied."

He closed his eyes and let out a ragged breath. *Way to state the obvious, Josie.*

"We'll work on that," she said in a whisper.

She started to unfasten her bustier, her gaze never leaving him. The garment fell around her ankles and she stood in front of him in nothing but her black lace panties, thigh-high hose and high heels. She trailed her fingers along the full undersides of her breasts, over her erect nipples, then downward, until they dipped inside her panties.

Immediately his erection strained to be inside her. He heard his own breath coming out in shallow pants.

She straddled him again, this time careful not to let their bodies come together. With one hand slowly massaging between her legs and the other gently caressing her own breast, she let her eyes close and her head fall back.

Trent gasped, "Please…"

But she ignored him. Her pelvis began to gently rock to her own rhythm, and as her breathing quickened she opened her eyes slightly and watched him watching her.

Trent's heart raced as he witnessed the irresistible show, and he strained against the cuffs again, his penis rigid and begging to be inside her. She stopped massaging between her legs and brought one of her still-damp fingers to her lips and tasted. Then she offered her finger to him.

"Would you like to taste how hot and wet I am?" she whispered.

He took her finger into his mouth and savored the taste of her. His cock throbbed with each heartbeat.

She leaned over and brought her lips to his ear. "Would you like to be inside of me now?"

Trent closed his eyes, admitted to himself that it was time to surrender. To hell with revenge. He wanted Josie.

"Yes," he said. "I want to be inside you."

JOSIE COULDN'T DO IT. Trent's acceptance of her intimate invitation brought reality home to her. No longer was this just an elaborate tease game, no longer could she ignore the truth. Here they were, about to have sex finally, after all these years.

She was terrified.

Visualize, Josie. Visualize.

She closed her eyes for a moment and inhaled deeply. The mental image she'd formed earlier of making love to Trent popped into her head, and she focused on it.

You can do this. You won't run away this time.

Josie opened her eyes and found Trent watching her. Only inches away. She tilted her head and planted a hungry kiss on his lips.

Yes, finally, she would have Trent.

She ached with a need so great it caused her hands and knees to tremble as she stood to rid herself of her panties and to take a condom from her bag. Then she climbed back onto Trent's lap. She fumbled to remove the condom from its wrapper, hoping she appeared more expert at the task than she felt. When she slid it over his erection as if she knew exactly what she was doing, she breathed a sigh of relief.

She shifted and felt his rock-hard penis press against her. With another slight shift of her hips, he was gliding inside. She savored the stretching, the sweet force of his body entering hers. It was even better than she'd imagined.

Trent gasped as she began to move her hips. She kissed him deep and long, letting their moaning and breathing intermingle until it was impossible to tell who had made a sound.

She was doing it! She'd conquered her fear, she realized suddenly, and just as quickly as the coherent thought came to her, it disappeared in a fog of heavenly sensations.

They were one, as she imagined soul mates became when they made love. Their bodies fit perfectly together, bonded by pleasure, the heat between them creating a chemical reaction of unimaginable proportions.

She experimented with her newfound power, moving quickly and then slowly, bringing Trent close to climax and then pulling back, while they took turns exploring each other with their mouths.

"You're killing me," he said when Josie quickened

the pace one last time, unable to take the anticipation any longer.

She clung to Trent as she felt herself coming closer to release, coming so fast it was nearly impossible to slow down.

Trent let his head fall back against the chair, his breathing ragged and shallow. "I'm going to come," he whispered.

"Me, too," Josie found the sense to say just before her muscles began to contract around him.

She held on tight to him, crying out, insensible, lost.

His climax came then, too, and he muffled their gasps with another kiss, this one desperate and searching.

After their release, they sat, still locked together, Josie draped over Trent's shoulder, their bodies spent.

She'd been right all these years. Making love to Trent was everything she'd been afraid of. It was a complete loss of control, even when she had him bound to a chair.

And it was better than she could have imagined.

When they recovered, she let him out of the handcuffs and he led her to the bedroom. As they explored each other's bodies together this time, equally in control, Josie marveled that Trent seemed to be a fast learner. He knew his way around her body like an expert, not a fumbling novice in need of sex lessons.

She deserved some sort of teaching award, if all Trent's newfound skills were thanks to their few lessons together. She was one heck of a sex instructor. But she had a nagging feeling that wasn't the whole story. There was something Trent wasn't telling her. Whatever it was, she'd get it out of him eventually.

There were always the handcuffs.

They made love slowly one more time, and once more after that, then fell asleep in each other's arms.

She awoke later to the sound of a cat howling outside somewhere. She watched Trent sleeping, tried to imagine what it would be like if they were there as two people in love, not as a student and instructor. An emptiness filled her chest, so she forced her thoughts to something more positive.

She'd done it!

The fact that she and Trent had finally made love was hard to completely wrap her mind around, but still, she'd gotten past that fear. There was no stopping her now. Josie smiled and stretched. Finally, her dry spell had come to an end. She had a sex life again, one better than she'd ever imagined.

She slipped out of bed and padded quietly across the floor to the bathroom. Trent's steady breathing was the only sound in the darkened apartment. She flipped on a light and closed the door quickly and silently to avoid waking him.

In the mirror, she saw that her lipstick was gone and she had a faint red rash around her mouth from Trent's five o'clock shadow. Her hair stood out around her head, giving her the mussed look of a mental patient, and a little voice in her head shouted, *That's exactly what you are!*

Reality came crashing in. She'd just traded sex for the *rent!* She could hardly recognize herself as the woman she'd been earlier, clad in black lace and bent on seduction. Somewhere along the way, between gathering up her "lesson materials" and handcuffing Trent to the chair, all her common sense had flown straight out the window.

Yet her body felt intensely relaxed. She would have loved to curl up with Trent and sleep until morning, but that would require her to face him in the clear light of day. She wasn't ready to face the man with whom she'd had to take such extreme measures to get into bed.

Josie turned the faucet on low and splashed cold water on her face. The icy water sent chills through her. When she felt sufficiently alert, she dried her face, switched the light off and ventured out into the apartment to search for her discarded clothes.

The garments formed a trail across the living room, leading Josie closer and closer to the door as she gathered up the lingerie. Pulling a street outfit out of her duffel bag to wear home, she finished dressing and carried her bag to the door.

When she unlocked it and stepped into the cold night air, she felt a momentary urge to stay. But no, she had to go.

The clock in her car read four minutes past midnight. Time for her to go home to rest up for work the next day. But Josie knew the wired feeling she had now meant insomnia, and there would be no point in trying to sleep. She'd left her laptop at work, and on it were her spreadsheets and other business documents. She could use her sleepless night to get some work done, so she made a right turn and headed toward the center.

When Josie pulled up to the curb, she spotted a light on in the hallway of the building. She didn't remember leaving it on, but it wasn't unusual for Erika to leave a light on at night to discourage burglars. Not that they had anything there worth stealing, Josie mused as she unlocked the front door and locked it again behind her.

Inside, Eros was nowhere in sight. She slipped off her shoes to avoid frightening him into hiding at the sound of her footsteps on the hardwood floors, then padded quietly down the hallway.

Her breath caught in her throat when she reached the

doorway of the office. There, sitting at the desk, was her mother.

"Wha—!" Josie shrieked, not even sure what she meant to say.

Rafaela, who'd had her head bent as she read a document on the desk, started and let out a gasp.

"What are you doing here?" Josie found the sense to ask.

"Josephine! You scared me half to death."

"Mother! Why aren't you in Prague?"

Rafaela leaned back in her chair and placed a hand on her chest, then exhaled noisily. "I decided to come back early, that's all."

"Without telling me? When? How? What happened?" Josie's mind raced as she sat on the sofa opposite the desk.

Eros sat perched next to Rafaela, a smug cat smile plastered across his mouth. No one was ever happier to see her than him.

She noted that her mother looked a little tired and puffy—natural side effects of the long flight back from Prague—but even after such a grueling trip, she was still unmistakably attractive. Her wild curly mane of nearly black hair was pulled back into a thick ponytail at her nape, and her pale skin, barely wrinkled after a lifetime of avoiding the sun, practically glowed in the lamplight. Even on a bad day, her mother could turn heads with her dancer's figure. And when she set her stunning blue gaze on a man, she could usually be assured he'd fall to his knees.

Rafaela removed her reading glasses and rubbed her eyes. "I'm afraid things didn't work out between Peter and me. It was better that I just leave immediately. There was no time to call you."

"But when did you get home?" Relief flooded Josie now that she'd recovered from the shock.

This meant her mother could take over the center again, get business back to normal. It meant Josie could look for another marriage counseling job, and she could call off her lessons with Trent immediately. That was all what she wanted, wasn't it? Of course it was.

"I just flew in this evening. I wanted to come by here and check on things. I hadn't anticipated your showing up and scaring me half to death."

"Why didn't you call me to come pick you up?"

Rafaela dismissed that idea with the wave of a hand. "I didn't want to bother you."

Josie smiled. "That's silly, but it's great to have you back. When do you plan to come back to work?"

Her mother frowned and stroked the cat. "Dear, I don't think I'll be coming back to run the center again."

"You mean, for a few weeks or so, right?"

"I mean, ever. I've spent a lot of years running this place, and frankly, I'm burnt out. I'd hoped you'd develop an interest in carrying on with the business without me."

Josie blinked, and blinked again. This was all wrong. Her mother couldn't be abandoning the center completely. She'd been working nonstop for three months now, hoping to salvage her mother's legacy, and for nothing?

"You can't just quit!"

"I'm fifty years old. I've earned the right to do whatever I want to do. Even if it means retiring early."

"But you'll get bored. You'll whither away. You'll hate retirement."

"I didn't say I wasn't going to work at all. I just don't intend to run this entire business any longer."

Josie slumped back into the couch, the wind knocked out of her. All this time she'd assumed her mother would come back and take over again. And now, the future of the center rested entirely on Josie's feeble shoulders.

TRENT STARED at the note, barely legible in Max's shaky script. MegaBooks had called again about buying the property. "We're prepared to increase our offer," the note read, followed by a phone number. The MegaBooks offer was a proposition he'd carefully avoided thinking about in the past few days, as complex as the implications were.

And now…

It had been two days since he and Josie had made love. Two days he'd spent examining the emotions that had sprung up in his chest since he'd begun spending time with her. Those emotions had only deepened with their lovemaking. It still seemed impossible that they'd finally done it. All his fantasies paled in comparison to Josie, live in the flesh and in his bed.

He'd tried to call her after she'd sneaked out of his apartment, but she hadn't returned his calls. He'd tried to stop by to see her, but she'd always managed to be out.

Okay, so his revenge plot was pretty much a failure. He had lost his will for it, anyway. It was hard to exact revenge on the woman he was falling for.

There. He'd let the thought form completely in his brain. He was falling for Josie again. God help him, but he was. Maybe he'd never gotten over his feelings from years ago. That would explain why her rejection of him had hurt so much.

If he could only figure out what to do with his emotions now. Josie didn't seem to be interested in anything more than a sexual relationship, but his heart was telling him there was something between them worth exploring.

All of a sudden the idea of leaving San Francisco and leading adventure tours full-time wasn't so appealing, if it meant never seeing Josie. He couldn't even think about the MegaBooks offer without getting a sick feeling in his gut.

"Dude, you look like you've got some deep thoughts rolling around in there," Max said.

Trent shook his head. "Just spacing out, that's all."

He tucked the note under the edge of the cash register, then came around the counter and turned his attention back to adjusting the brakes on a mountain bike he'd just sold. The customer was supposed to come back in an hour to pick it up, just as soon as Trent fitted it with the extra equipment the man had bought.

Max kept staring at him. "Hey, man, you just get laid recently or something?"

"Why do you ask?"

"You been acting like you've had your brain fried by a hot piece of ass."

Trent tested the brakes. "That's a classy way of putting it."

"Watch out, dude. Let a woman get control of you, you're a goner."

"Thanks for the advice. Now could you go see if that customer needs help?" Trent nodded at a teenager near the front of the store.

"Already checked. He's just looking."

"Then how about you go restock water bottles or wander out into traffic or something?"

"Man, you are whipped, aren't you?" Max grinned

and took a seat on the counter, settling in to annoy Trent some more.

Trent scowled at him. "Last time I checked, you didn't exactly have women lined up to take control of your life."

"Hey, at least I admit I'm a fool for women. But I'm twenty-two years old. What guy my age isn't?"

"I see, and as an old geezer of thirty years, I should have all women figured out by now."

"You shouldn't have that whipped look in your eyes—that's all I'm saying."

Trent bit his lip, unable to think of a smart-ass comeback. How had he, in a matter of days, gone from having his life under complete control to looking so pitiful that even Max, who was normally about as perceptive as a rock, could see there was something wrong?

Josie Marcus had walked back into his life—that's what had gone wrong.

As if on cue, someone walked into the store. Trent looked up to see Josie. In a sort of lavender-colored suit, with her wild, wavy hair pulled back into some kind of professional woman's hairdo, she looked like every man's boardroom fantasy, the sex-pot CEO.

"Max, get lost."

The store clerk eyed him, then Josie, with interest as she made her way down the aisle toward them. "Ah, so she's the one," he said in a stage whisper.

Trent glowered and Max got the message. He hopped off the counter and disappeared into the stockroom just as Josie stopped on the other side of the mountain bike. She stared down at Trent as he kneeled on the floor, making one last adjustment to the brakes. When he finished, he stood and officially acknowledged her presence for the first time.

She smiled tentatively. "I know my timing is awful, but we need to talk about the other night."

It's about time.

"How about we go for a walk?" he said.

Josie nodded, and Trent called to the back for Max. When the clerk appeared in the doorway of the stockroom, Trent said, "I'll be back in a little while. Can you take care of everything until I get back?"

"No problem, man," Max answered. When Josie turned toward the front door, he eyed her and smiled, then nodded knowingly.

Outside they made a left and walked toward the Pacific, which was more than twenty blocks away. It could still be seen on high ground, though, glinting in the distance. And the smell of it always permeated the air. Trent couldn't think of many things he loved more than the scent of the ocean.

"So…" Josie said, clearly hesitant to dive into a discussion of their newfound sexual relationship.

"So." Trent didn't intend to let her off the hook easily after she'd snuck out of his bed without saying goodbye.

"Did you know my mother is back from Prague?"

"Rafaela's *here?*"

Trent went numb at the thought that his sex lessons with Josie could be over for good.

"She showed up unannounced the other night, claiming things didn't work out between her and Peter."

"I guess that solves all your problems, then," Trent said.

"Actually, everything is worse now than I thought. My mother doesn't want to run the center at all anymore!"

"She expects you to run it from now on?" His imagination automatically conjured the idea of a permanent sex-lessons-for-rent trade.

"Yes, and she's crazy. I'm awful at running that place."

"You seem to be doing pretty well with a business that was in near ruins when you took it over."

"It's still in near ruins—you call that doing pretty well?"

"You're not giving yourself credit. And maybe Rafaela will stick around as an advisor."

Josie frowned. "Maybe, but she'll have to advise someone else."

Trent shrugged. "Your decision."

They fell into an awkward silence as they waited for a light to change so they could cross a street. Trent forced himself not to make small talk, to force Josie to address the subject they were dancing around. The light turned green and they crossed the street.

She finally spoke up. "I just want you to know, I'm sorry for what happened the other night. I should never had tied you to the chair and…and—"

Trent interrupted, his gut clenching at the thought that she considered the night an unfortunate accident. "It's not like you forced me. I was a consenting adult."

"But still, I feel like I coerced you." She watched her feet as she walked. "I hope this doesn't cancel our professional arrangement."

"You mean, the sex lessons?"

"Yes."

"Why would it? Like you said, I'll never learn anything without hands-on experience." Trent was careful to keep his voice free of emotion.

"That's true, I guess."

"You just helped me get past that hang-up I had, my fear of performing for you," he lied.

Josie nodded. "Yes, you seem to have overcome the performance anxiety right away."

Oops. Maybe if he hadn't been crazy with desire, he could have put on more of an act, but Josie had made acting difficult, if not impossible.

"Let's just say your, uh, lesson was exactly what I needed."

"Good, I'm glad." She paused, seeming to search for the right words. "And I'm sorry I slipped out without saying goodbye afterward."

"Why did you?"

"I just woke up and…it seemed like the next morning could be awkward, us being student and teacher. It seemed like it would be unprofessional for me to spend the night, and I didn't want to wake you."

Trent resisted pointing out that their entire arrangement was the polar opposite of professional.

"No big deal," he lied.

"I should have left a note."

"Maybe a little evaluation sheet, with grades for performance and effort."

Josie smiled. "A-plus-plus."

"For performance, or effort?"

"Both. You hardly seemed like you needed sex lessons."

"I've got a great instructor."

She laughed. "So we're still on for next week?"

"Of course."

"And you'll still help me with the business assessment and the weekend retreat?"

Trent stopped walking and placed a hand on her arm. "We have a deal, and I won't break it."

"I'm so glad you're okay with all this. The center would be financially ruined for sure without our arrangement." She stood on tiptoe and placed a kiss on his cheek. "Thank you so much!"

"No problem."

"I have to get back to the center. So I'll see you next Tuesday." She was walking backward, getting farther away from him now. She lifted her hand to wave, and when he nodded she turned and walked away.

Trent stood alone on the sidewalk, suddenly aware of the salty fish smell coming from the sushi joint on his left. He watched Josie's retreating form, and with each step she took, the knot in his gut grew bigger.

Would Josie always retreat from him? Was she incapable of doing anything else? Would she ever have slept with him if not for financial necessity? Part of him wanted to hang around long enough to find out. Another part suddenly wanted to tell MegaBooks he was ready to accept their offer.

9

HEAVEN HELP HER, Josie was turning into her mother.

Her old fear came surging back, stronger than ever, only this time she knew it was completely warranted. She *was* capable of losing control, of letting her passions rule her, of letting desire for a particularly sexy man control her life.

She gnawed on a pen, staring at the syllabus in front of her. She'd written it up the day Trent had made his offer of trading sex lessons for the rent. At the time the solution had seemed ideal. Half crazed by her lack of a sex life, she'd designed every lesson to give herself plenty of opportunities to get Trent into bed for hands-on practice.

She saw now that she'd been doing the kinds of things she'd always disliked Rafaela doing. Chasing after men, thinking constantly about sex, letting her libido guide her decision-making… Was this kind of behavior genetically passed down from mother to daughter?

Suddenly the sex-heavy lessons she'd devised didn't seem like such a fabulous idea. She just wasn't cut out for casual sex.

She tried to close her mind's eye to the events of their last lesson, but every time she let her guard down, the erotic images replayed themselves over and over again in her mind. Her brain had become an X-rated movie theater.

She couldn't even recall why she'd thought she could pull off seducing Trent without a hitch. She'd let pure desperation blind her to the inevitable aftereffects.

She was no better than her mother. The thought filled her with the urge to change her name and move to Peru, perhaps to join an order of contemplative nuns.

Ah, but if she dwelled on thoughts of Trent for more than a few seconds, her entire body awakened to desire again.

Eros awoke from his favorite spot atop the leather sofa and came trotting over to the desk. He'd developed such a liking for living at the center, Rafaela had decided to leave him there until she could get the carpets in her condo cleaned. She claimed he always freaked out and hid in the closet for days after the carpet-cleaning men came with their noisy steam cleaners and she wanted to save him the trauma.

In one smooth, feline leap Eros positioned himself right in front of Josie on the desktop. And in an unprecedented show of friendliness, he began to purr in deep rumbles and to butt his head up against Josie's face. She sneezed and tried to pick the cat hair out of her mouth discreetly enough so as not to offend him.

"Does this mean you like me now?" Josie ran her hand along his silky back, but he ducked away from her touch.

When someone knocked on the office door, he bolted and disappeared under the sofa.

Josie blinked at the cat's odd behavior, then called for her visitor to come in.

Erika poked her head inside the doorway. "You have a few minutes to talk?"

Josie glanced down at the calendar on her desk, with its column of empty lines for Thursday. "Uh, sure."

Erika stepped into the office and closed the door behind her. Today she was wearing lots of crushed velvet and gold jewelry, complete with sandals that wound their way up her calves, and toe rings on several toes.

"Please, have a seat." Josie motioned to a chair across from her, but Erika had already flopped into it before she could finish the sentence. "What's up?"

"We need to talk about my future here at the center."

"Is something wrong? You know you have a job here as long as we're in business."

"I don't want to be a receptionist forever." Erika crossed her arms over her chest and flashed Josie a look of challenge.

"I've learned a lot from Rafaela over the years, and I think I should get a chance to contribute something more than my phone-answering skills to this business."

Josie tried to hide her surprise. She wasn't sure why she'd never considered the possibility herself, as desperate as she'd been lately. The only problem was, aside from her massage therapy, Erika didn't have any qualifications that she knew of—and Josie wasn't prepared to offer massage through the center. "That's an interesting idea. Where do you feel your expertise is?"

"My official title could be Sex Coach. I may not have formal training, but I know I have the necessary skills. And I've got a hunch this will be the next big thing in couples therapy."

"*Sex* coaching?"

"There are already lifestyle coaches and weight-loss coaches. Why not sex coaches and marriage coaches? The idea of going to a coach attracts people who wouldn't want to see a therapist, either because of the stigma attached, or because they don't consider themselves that dysfunctional. But just about anyone could see themselves using a coach for some area of their life.''

Wow, she really had something there. Josie sat back in her chair to consider the possibilities.

"Okay, let's say we start advertising your services through the center. What qualifies you to be a sex coach?"

"My expertise. I've got a sixth sense about how people are screwing up their lives, especially when it comes to issues of the bedroom."

"Oh?"

"Let's take you, for example. I'd guess you're in desperate need of a sex coach."

"What makes you think that?" Josie asked, sinking down in her seat a little.

"I see how distracted and flaky you've been lately. You've got major issues with our hunky landlord, much more serious than you first led me to believe."

"Things between us are...complicated."

"So try me. If I can give you some useful advice for your problems with Trent, you give me a chance as the center's first sex coach."

Josie weighed the possible benefits against the humiliation of explaining her arrangement with Trent. She had nothing to lose except her pride. "Okay, you have a deal, but I like the title Sensuality Coach better. So how, exactly, do we get started?"

"Don't look so worried. It's painless. I just coach you on how to improve your sex life, then we develop a game plan on how to set things right, and you check back in with me periodically so I can make sure you stay on the right track."

"You've got this pretty well thought out."

Erika frowned. "Don't sound so surprised. I've been researching this idea for months."

"I'm impressed."

"Go ahead then, give me a summary of what's been going on between you and Trent up to this point."

Josie hesitated. "I don't know. I think I can just work this out on my own."

"Really?" Erika said as if Josie had just claimed to have written the Kama Sutra. "Going it alone is what got you into this predicament."

True, but she didn't have to be so snide about it.

"Okay, fine." Josie gulped. Could she really divulge every last pitiful detail of her relationship with Trent to a woman she had to work with day in and day out? Sadly, she was just desperate enough to try it.

After all, if Erika was really good, she could be the factor that put the center back on track. Who knew what the key to saving the business might be—even a self-styled sex coach.

Josie swallowed her modesty and began.

She started with the Ocean Beach incident three years ago, filling in the details Erika wasn't familiar with, then skipped forward to the day when Trent walked back into her life. She explained their arrangement, their series of near misses, and finally her hand-cuffing him to a chair and making love to him.

Erika listened intently, offering an occasional "Hmm" or "I see."

When Josie finished her sad tale, Erika sat back in her chair and expelled a weary sigh. "It's even worse than I thought."

"It is?"

"You, my dear boss, are a mess."

"I think we've already established that. So fix me."

Erika smoothed her green-velvet dress over her legs. She pursed her lips, apparently deep in thought. Either that or pondering how best to break the news that Josie was a lost cause.

"Let me make sure I understand this correctly... *He* asked *you* for sex lessons."

"That's so hard to believe?"

"Men rarely admit inadequacy in the bedroom."

She had a point there.

Erika stared at Josie speculatively. "It sounds to me like Trent is stringing you along. Is he the vengeful type?"

Trent? Vengeful? Not under ordinary circumstances, but...

Josie thought about their lessons thus far, the odd reasons he gave for backing out of sex at the last second, the amazing skill he'd demonstrated in bringing her just to the edge of orgasm before she'd taken control of the situation.

Vengeance. Josie rolled the concept around in her head. Could it be that Trent was getting even with her for Ocean Beach? Impossible. Or was it? Now that she thought about it...

It made perfect sense.

Yes. That had to be it. How could she have not seen it herself?

"Oh. Wow. You're right." A stab of anger penetrated Josie's middle, but just as quickly as it appeared, it disappeared. How could she be angry at Trent for giving her exactly what she deserved? She was, after all, the one who'd ditched him in the first place, leaving him humiliated and without underwear on the beach. If she'd been in his shoes, she might have done the same or worse.

"I told you I'm good at this stuff." Erika smiled triumphantly. "My talents are endless."

"That must make life simple for you."

She ignored Josie's sarcasm. "Now that you know his secret, you can use it to your advantage."

"To what end?" Josie couldn't imagine what hope there was for her relationship with Trent.

"What exactly do you want out of your liaison with this guy you've forcibly seduced?"

"I didn't forcibly seduce him! I just sort of, well, encouraged things along a bit. With handcuffs."

Okay, so she'd "forcibly seduced" him.

"Answer my question. What do you want from Trent?"

Oh, right. What the heck did she want from him? Hot sex obviously hadn't satisfied her the way she'd hoped it would. And the thought that he was trying to exact revenge on her changed everything. It had become all too clear that she could no longer continue in the present with Trent without facing their past.

"I suppose I just want to get through the remaining lessons with him without making a fool of myself or developing a sexual addiction to him," she said, trying to ignore the vague feeling that she'd just told a lie.

Erika scrunched up her thin black eyebrows and frowned. "You have a young virile male at your command, and that's the best goal you can come up with? See what I mean? You're a mess."

"He and I are all wrong for each other. I just don't want to string him along."

"Why do you think he's all wrong for you?"

"I don't like gorgeous men. And I don't like men who make me think about sex all the time."

"I suppose you also hate chocolate."

Josie watched as Eros came slinking out from under the couch, crossed the floor to Erika, rubbing against her leg and purring like a sports car.

"You said his favorite word—chocolate," she explained.

The cat settled in at Erika's feet and began kneading the rug with his paws.

She scratched his head. "Sorry, buddy, I don't have any of the good stuff for you."

"I don't see what my taste in men has to do with chocolate," Josie said, beginning to wish her new sex coach would get the hell out of her office.

"My advice to you is, let your libido be your guide. If you're strongly attracted to Trent, put aside your silly reservations and see what happens with him."

"And then my sex life will improve?"

"He obviously has strong feelings for you or he never would have sought vengeance for your past misdeeds against him."

Strong feelings? Trent? Impossible.

Josie laughed. "No, he's just competitive. He probably couldn't stand to have me one up on him."

"Don't be so sure about that. His is a pretty elaborate scheme, too elaborate for simple competitiveness."

"If you say so." She knew Trent, though. In high school he'd always pursued girls until they'd fallen for him, then he lost interest. It was his game, and she knew better than to play along with it.

"It doesn't make you mad that he's out for revenge?"

"No... Well, maybe a little, but I can't say I don't deserve it."

"You're sure you want him as a lover?"

Did she?

But no sooner did the question form in her mind than she knew the answer. Yes, yes, yes. She wanted Trent in her bed. Knowing his scheme only made her want him more. A perverse impulse, but there it was.

Josie had been trying to convince herself, ever since they'd had sex, that she didn't. That simply by denying her desire for Trent she could be nothing like her mother.

But she'd been lying to herself. "Yes, I do."

TRENT LOOKED at his watch. He was supposed to be meeting Josie for their lesson tonight and here was his dad, Mr. Lonely Heart, camped out in Trent's kitchen, looking pitiful. He'd been cooking all day, judging by the state of the kitchen, a sure sign that he was still feeling blue. Now he was washing a sinkful of dishes Trent hadn't even been aware he owned.

Trent felt a pang of guilt for not spending more time with his dad lately, when he knew he probably needed some companionship. He'd let his lust for Josie dominate his waking thoughts and he'd been a lousy son. Even if his father did put a crimp in his plans when he'd shown up unannounced, Trent could have been more flexible. He could have been a hell of a lot more sympathetic.

Between Josie's mother and Trent's father, they were going to have to join a children-of-middle-aged-parents support group.

Her mother and his father...

There was an idea. Crazy, but still... The two were perfect for each other. Both single, middle-aged, eccentric, loved to travel, drove their kids nuts. Trent had always liked Rafaela. He wondered why he'd never taken the match seriously before. The only problem was, how to convince the two parents to get together.

"You want something to eat?" his dad asked, a skillet in hand.

"No, thanks. I have dinner plans."

"Oh, a hot date?"

"Something like that."

"Always so private, you. Just once I want to meet one of these girls you go out with. Good thing I'm here tonight, I can meet this one. What's her name?"

"Her name's Josie. But this isn't serious, so don't get any ideas in your head."

"What you need is to find a nice girl to settle down with."

"You're one to talk."

His father flashed him an indignant look. "I had twenty-five good years with your mother. We got married young, but that's what kids did in those days. I never regretted a thing."

Good years? Trent has always assumed his dad looked back on his marriage with regret, that he'd missed the passion their marriage lacked. His recent skirt-chasing behavior had done little to discourage that theory. Rather, it had tarnished his mother's memory, and that made Trent angry.

"I didn't think you were happy with Mom." A stab of pain sliced through Trent's gut. He'd come to terms with his mother's death, but he'd never completely gotten used to it, and occasionally the brutal reality of it hit him anew.

His father shot him a look of disbelief. "We had our problems, but your mother was my best friend. There's not a day goes by that I don't miss her."

Trent blinked. He'd never discussed this subject with

his dad before, and maybe he'd made too many assumptions. Now that he thought about it, he had to admit that what his parents had lacked in passion, they'd made up for in other ways—strong friendship, happy family life, shared interests.

He suddenly got the feeling he'd been looking at relationships from the wrong angle all along.

Trent hadn't met a woman yet that he could envision himself having a happy marriage with—passionate or not. He sometimes doubted he ever would, and occasionally, that thought bothered the hell out of him. Other times, he figured he was lucky not to have to endure the pain of losing a loved one all over again.

"Are you seeing someone now?"

His father waved a hand in the air. "Women—who needs 'em."

"Why did you break up with that last girl?"

He frowned, drying his hands on a towel. "She stole money from my wallet."

"Sounds like you had yourself a real winner."

"Hey, she was cute. That's all I knew." He pulled out a chair and took a seat at the table.

"I know someone I think you'd like."

"Oh, yeah? She got big knockers?"

This was the kind of thing that made Trent less than thrilled at times to have his dad around. "That's not exactly a politically correct way to say it."

"So does she?"

Trent cringed. "She has a nice figure."

"How old?"

"Does it matter?"

"I don't want some divorcée on the rebound. They spend the whole night complaining about their exes."

"She's not a recent divorcée, and she's about your age, maybe a little younger."

"Why are you so interested in fixing me up all of a sudden?"

"I think you'd like this woman, that's all."

His dad shrugged. "Okay. Why not? Introduce us."

That had been easy—too easy. His dad must have been even lonelier that Trent had first suspected.

He grabbed the cordless phone from the wall and went into the bedroom to call Josie. The phone rang three times before she picked up with a breathless "Hello?"

"Hey, it's me. What're you doing, running a marathon?"

"No." Her voice dropped to a whisper. "I had to run for the phone before my mom picked it up. I didn't want her to hear if it was you."

"Don't want her to know about us?"

"I don't want her getting the wrong idea, thinking we're an item when we're not."

His stomach twisted and he told himself it was just his pride that smarted at the thought that Josie didn't want them to be "an item."

"Sure, makes sense. I'm calling because my dad is moping around my apartment, and I hate to leave him here alone like this. I was thinking, your mom...my dad..."

"I'm listening." From the sound of her voice, he could picture the perplexed crease forming across her forehead.

"Maybe we could fix them up."

"Oh. Jeez, I don't know. I mean, I can't remember the last time my mother dated someone her own age."

"Yeah, well, same for my dad. They're perfect for each other."

Josie sighed. "She hates matchmaking."

"So we'll make her think their meeting is accidental."

"But how?"

Right—how?

"Uh, invite her to dinner with you tonight. I'll take my dad along, and you guys will walk by our table and you can act like you're just bumping into us. Then we'll invite you to join us."

"Hmm. But what about our lesson?"

"I'll buy you dinner instead, and we'll reschedule the lesson."

"Isn't that breaching our student-teacher relationship?" she said, her tone teasing.

"Most student-teacher relationships don't involve sex lessons, so I think we can make up the rules as we go."

"And our rules allow dinner on you?"

"Absolutely."

"Tell me where you want to meet, then I'll call you back to let you know if I can talk my mom into dinner."

"How about that new Italian place on Irving?"

"Trattoria Venezia?"

"That's it."

"Okay, I'll call you back in a few."

Trent disconnected and sank back on his bed. He stretched his arms over his head and closed his eyes, indulging in thoughts of what he'd hoped to be doing on his bed tonight. Images of Josie, the arch of her back, the fullness of her breasts, the honey-colored triangle of curls he longed to bury his face in... He groaned and sat up. No, if he kept on thinking like that he'd have to kick his dad out on the streets and drag Josie in here pronto.

What he needed was patience, distraction, a bucket of ice down his pants.

The phone rang and he snapped it up and pressed the on button. "Hello?"

"She's up for dinner. But this has to be authentic looking. If she suspects it's a setup, she'll never go for it."

"I'll see you there around seven-thirty then?"

"That's fine." Her voice dropped an octave lower. "Oh, and by the way, I was looking forward to our lesson tonight. Just so you know, I won't be wearing any underwear." And with that she hung up the phone.

Trent flopped back on the bed and let out a frustrated groan. Another month of this temptation and he'd go insane.

JOSIE HAD NEVER FELT so scandalous in her life. Sure, she'd done some pretty eye-popping things in the past month with Trent, but that was all in the name of his sensual development.

None of it felt nearly as scandalous as walking down a San Francisco street with no underwear on, the breeze whipping at her bare lower half. She'd chosen a short, body-hugging black dress for the occasion, the sort of outfit she decided a woman who didn't wear underwear would choose. And of course, that outfit would not be complete without a pair of black heels, the kind with straps that wound up around the ankles.

Okay, so having her mother in tow sort of dampened her bad-girl mood. But as they made their way to the restaurant, Josie entertained herself with thoughts of what she would do with Trent once she finally got him to admit his feelings for her. Oh, the scandalous things they would do...

Thanks to Erika, Josie understood Trent more than she ever had before. Erika had a surprising talent for this sex coaching stuff. She'd told Josie to avoid having sex with Trent again until they'd resolved their conflicts and admitted their true feelings for each other. It was sound advice, and remarkably simple, if not exactly simple to execute.

For tonight, anyway, Josie was going to assume that foreplay—really intense foreplay—was still okay.

"Josephine, would you please stop walking so fast?"

"Sorry." She slowed to match her mother's pace, annoyed with herself for being in such a hurry to see Trent.

"I'm surprised you can move so fast in those shoes. What are you doing dressed for a night on the town, anyway, when you're just entertaining your mother?"

Darn it, she shouldn't have been so obvious. "I need to make a trip to the cleaner's. This is about the only clean dress I have left."

"Well, you look fabulous in it. You should choose more outfits that accent your figure like that."

Leave it to her mother to compliment her on wearing the sort of dress that would keep most parents up late worrying. Josie used to wish she had a normal mother who baked cookies and drove her to Girl Scout meetings, but now she more or less accepted that Rafaela wasn't ever going to be normal.

"I had a meeting with Erika the other day regarding her future at the center, and I've decided that she should have more responsibility than she currently does."

"Erika's a smart girl," Rafaela said. "I've been trying to think of better ways to use her recently."

"She's going to be our sex—er, sensuality—coach. We need to start advertising it."

"A sensuality coach! That's a fabulous idea."

"Erika's, not mine."

"I'm sure you can handle the advertising," Rafaela said, clearly finished with the subject.

Josie clenched her teeth to avoid making any comment. She had given up trying to get her mother more involved in running the center again, but she still found her lack of interest frustrating.

Even more frustrating was her lack of explanation for any of her recent odd behavior. She hadn't returned any money to the business account, hadn't shown the slightest worry about the shaky finances at the center, and now suddenly she claimed to be burnt out on a job she'd adored up until a few months ago?

Josie was beginning to suspect more and more that her mother had an ulterior motive. Rafaela was manipulating her somehow, but her reasons weren't clear. And Josie was so overwhelmed with the day-to-day details of running the center that she didn't have the mental or physical energy to figure out what was really going on with her mother.

She just had to hope that, eventually, everything would work out.

They found Trattoria Venezia and Josie tried to look nonchalant as they entered the small restaurant and immediately spotted Trent and his father sitting at one of the tables closest to the door.

Rafaela smiled and waved, and Josie let out a pent-up breath, relieved that her mother didn't seem to suspect any foul play at Trent's presence.

"Trent, dear, how nice to see you!"

"Hi, Rafaela. Back from Prague so soon?"

"Yes, I just couldn't stay away from San Francisco a moment longer."

She turned her attention to Trent's father, a faint look of recognition in her expression. "Tony O'Reilly?"

"Rafaela Marcus, I haven't seen you since—jeez, how long has it been?"

Her mother frowned. "Not since you gave up the sporting goods business, right?"

"Must be." Trent's father looked stunned and a little confused that his blind date had turned out to be not so blind, after all.

"We haven't ordered yet. Why don't you two join us?" Trent said, already standing and offering a chair to Josie's mother.

"Uh, that's okay with me. Mom?"

"If you're sure you don't mind."

Trent's father looked even more confused now, and he was eyeing Trent with mild curiosity. "We'd be happy to have you," he finally said, catching on to the plan that Trent must not have informed him about.

One good look at Trent sitting there in a crisp white shirt and khaki pants, and all those fantasies Josie'd been indulging in throughout the day came flooding back. Somehow, she had to get him out of here. Fast. Even if, according to Erika, she couldn't make love to Trent until he admitted his feelings, she could at least engage in a little extended foreplay.

All in the name of education, of course.

THEY MADE SMALL TALK while looking over the menus, and Josie calculated exactly how long she needed to wait before she and Trent could slip away to the rest room. Or the car. Or the nearest hotel room.

After the waiter took their order, Rafaela smiled and

asked Trent a few questions about his store. She was watching Trent and Josie closely, too closely. Josie feared her mother suspected this was a setup, after all.

And if so, she'd never hear the end of it.

But then Rafaela surprised her with, "Why don't you two give us old folks some time alone to get reacquainted? We can have the waiter box up your dinners for carry-out."

Trent and Josie exchanged a look. Trent's father, too, seemed a little taken aback by the suggestion.

"Uh," Josie said, stunned. "That's fine with me. Trent?"

He looked to Rafaela. "You sure you want to be stuck having dinner alone with this old coot?"

Her mother smiled and patted Tony's hand. "It's been a long time. We have lots to catch up on."

"I've gotta warn you, get him started talking about his boat and he'll keep you here until morning."

Rafaela signaled the waiter. When he arrived, she explained the change of plans.

They sat awkwardly sipping their drinks while Josie wondered about the smug look on her mother's face. And then, thankfully, their dinners came and Trent and Josie excused themselves.

Outside the restaurant they stopped and looked at one another in disbelief.

"What was *that* all about?" Trent asked.

"My mother's up to something."

"Do you think she suspects anything about us?"

"It's possible. Even if she doesn't, this might be her way of getting us together." Josie felt herself blushing to admit, "She's always insisted we'd make a perfect couple."

Josie suddenly had the feeling that her mother's odd

behavior in recent months was connected to some kind of elaborate matchmaking plot. Would she really go so far just to get Josie and Trent together?

Trent frowned. ''I wonder if she and my dad have some kind of history?''

''No way! My mother has never, ever shown an interest in a guy her own age. At least not since I've been old enough to tell.''

Josie ran through the possibility again in her head. The center had been located right next door to Anthony O'Reilly's business, but so what? Back then he hadn't owned the building where the center was located—Trent had bought it after taking over the store—so their contact with each other probably had been limited to passing on the sidewalk, exchanging hellos, maybe chatting about neighborhood business. But being attracted?

The possibility was just too weird to consider.

Besides, Trent's father had been married back then. And Rafaela, many faults as she had, abided by a strict policy of never messing with married men.

Trent looked relieved by Josie's assurance.

''So where should we go?'' he asked, holding up their bag of dinner. ''Your place or mine?''

Josie had left her car keys for her mother to take herself and Anthony home. ''Your apartment is closer.''

''Which place would be more conducive to tonight's lesson?''

''Oh, *that*.'' With Trent so near, and the possibilities so endless all of a sudden, Josie was having a hard time remembering what tonight's lesson was even supposed to have been. ''I left the lesson plan at home.''

He raised an eyebrow. ''Do you really need a lesson plan?''

"I like to be prepared."

"Can't you go by memory?"

"My memory tends to be, uh, a little shaky when you're around."

He slipped one arm around her waist and pulled her close. She could feel his breath on her face now, and her entire body warmed instantly.

"Oh, yeah? Why is that?" he asked.

Josie tried to think of what Erika would advise her to say. Honesty was the best policy, right?

"Because you turn me on."

10

EVER SINCE Trent had gotten a look at Josie in that formfitting little black dress and those strappy heels, he'd felt all his reservations about her vanish.

She sat on his lap, her pelvis firmly pressed against his erection, and the look in her eyes told him she meant to have him, one way or another. Something about Josie had changed, something fundamental. This couldn't be the flirty tease he'd grown up lusting after. She never would have let his hand go as far up her dress as it just had moments ago, to confirm she wore not a scrap of underwear.

Damn if he didn't want her more than he'd wanted a woman in years. Why did his lust always have to multiply by ten when Josie Marcus was involved?

She gave him a measured look. "Why don't you tell me what you'd like to learn tonight?"

Hmm. Decisions, decisions.

Trent mulled over the options, then suggested, "How about a lesson in foreplay? I've been giving that subject a lot of thought lately, and I even have a sort of extra credit project on it."

"You did a project for *me?*"

"You do accept extra credit, don't you?" he asked, teasing.

Josie shrugged, the corners of her mouth down-turned in a suspicious little frown. "I've never thought about it, but I guess I can't say no. My curiosity is certainly piqued.''

She bit her delicate pink lip, and the gesture was wildly erotic. He imagined those lips, swollen from teasing, tempting, tasting, kissing parts of him he'd bet Josie would never agree to kiss.

Well, the old Josie. This new Josie that had just hopped on his lap might have learned a thing or two in the past couple of years, may have even learned something from that ridiculous sex school.

Trent reached for the magazine on the end table and opened up the erotica short story collection. He flipped to the story he'd read at least twice since swiping the magazine from Josie's waiting area.

"Hey, where did you get that?"

"I found it at the center. I didn't think you'd mind if I borrowed it."

"I didn't realize you enjoyed women's erotica."

"It's part of my research into the female psyche."

"I bet."

"Oh, I almost forgot the most important part." He lifted her off his lap and stood, then went to the kitchen for matches and candles.

He'd bought just about every candle he'd seen at the store earlier. As he arranged them on the coffee table, Josie stared, wide-eyed.

"Okay, I'm impressed. You're the first guy I've ever met who had one scented candle in his apartment, let alone fifty of them."

"What can I say—I'm a Renaissance man."

She snuggled herself into the corner of the couch and watched as he lit each candle.

Trent turned off the overhead light to maximize the mood created by the blaze of candles. Then he settled in at the opposite end of the sofa from Josie and pulled her bare feet onto his lap.

"Tonight," Trent said, "I'll be doing an erotic reading."

She looked at him, then the magazine, then him again, her eyes wide. "Wow."

"Why so shocked?" He could hardly resist cracking a grin. Her reaction was even better than he'd imagined.

"You've been listening, haven't you?"

He shrugged. "To be honest, I got the idea from one of your students that day I dropped in on the elderly women's sex class."

"You *have* been listening."

Trent found the spot where he wanted to begin reading.

"'Sabine stretched out long upon the grass, her every sense on alert at the nearness of the stranger. Just as he had every afternoon for the past two weeks, he watched her. Watched as she disrobed at the edge of the lake, watched as she dipped her naked body into the cool green water, and watched still as she lay in the grass letting the sun dry her damp skin.'

"'Sabine grew more and more curious about him each day, so that when he finally emerged from behind the bushes, she felt as if she already knew him. He was younger than she'd imagined, perhaps even younger than herself. His body was strong, graceful and unblemished by age—a body made for pleasuring a woman.'"

Trent paused to wet his lips. "Ready for more?"

Josie wiggled her toes. "Mmm-hmm."

If he had to guess, he'd say she was loving every minute of it. Her attention was focused on him as if he were about to reveal a long-kept secret.

"'She couldn't take another moment of his watching.

The distance between them had become a field of electric current…'" Trent continued to read, glancing up occasionally to see Josie getting more hot and bothered as the story went on. He was having a similar reaction, and it surprised him that even he found the candles to be a turn-on.

When he finished the story Josie smiled. "A-plus on the extra-credit project. That's exactly the kind of foreplay women love."

"Oh, yeah?" Trent smiled and began to massage Josie's feet. "How about foot massage? Is that a good thing to do?"

She closed her eyes and moaned. "Definitely."

He worked slowly, paying attention to each foot, then moving upward. Her calves, her thighs, her hands, her arms, her shoulders.

Josie went limp, fully enjoying the massage. He rolled her onto her stomach, then worked on her back until his hands ached. The rest of his body ached, too, for an entirely different reason. The experience of having full access to Josie's body, without touching it in an overtly sexual way, was sweet torture.

When he stopped, she rolled over and sighed. "That was incredible."

He was kneeling on the floor next to the couch. Josie reached out and touched his brow, traced the scar on his left eyebrow, one he'd gotten at a baseball game when they were kids.

"I remember when this happened. You bled all over first base and Jimmy Santiago passed out at the sight of all that blood."

He laughed. "I forgot all about that. We teased Jimmy for years afterward."

"Is that why he stole your prom date?"

"Maybe."

He'd always told Josie that she had been his backup date. They'd argued over it a million times.

"Don't start in on prom just because I mentioned it," she said.

But he couldn't resist. "You were such a tease."

"Was not."

"You wouldn't even give me a good-night kiss. Other guys were losing their virginity, and I was going home to take a cold shower. What a prom date you were."

"You didn't deserve a kiss. I was your fourth-choice date!"

He grinned. "Well, that's what I told you back then, anyway."

She smiled. "Jerk."

"What can I say—I was a dumb teenager."

"Now there's something we can agree on." She laughed, pulled a pillow off the couch and walloped him with it.

Trent caught her arms and pinned them up over her head. "So, if I let you go, are you gonna get up and give me *my* massage now, or will I have to demonstrate my skill in the ancient art of tickling?"

Josie's eyes narrowed. "There's no such thing as a free massage, is there?"

His voice took on a husky tone as he whispered, "I can think of better things I could give you for free."

A slow smile spread across her lips. "Yeah? I'm waiting."

He secured her wrists in one hand and trailed the fingers of his other hand down her arm until he reached her breast. There, he lingered, tracing a slow spiral inward until he reached her nipple.

When he found her neck with his lips and sucked gently, she gasped and arched herself toward him. She was so ripe, so sweet, so tempting… No way he could resist. But if he didn't slow down, he'd never be able to act out the all-night seduction he'd started with the erotic reading and the massage.

He paused and flashed Josie a wicked look.

"What?" she asked, immediately suspicious.

"Oh…just this." And he launched into a tickle assault, buying himself a few minutes to regain his cool.

Josie screeched and tried to fight him off, but she was giggling too much to be any real threat. Trent climbed on top of her and went for her ribs, realizing too late that his new position, straddling her, wasn't exactly going to ease his desire. She wiggled and squirmed until the remaining cushions fell off the couch and her dress had worked its way up to reveal that she really wasn't wearing any underwear. Trent feared his zipper would burst from his straining erection.

"Uncle! Uncle!" Josie cried.

He stopped tickling but kept his fingers poised to continue if need be, while making a concerted effort not to stare at the sexy thatch of curls peaking out from beneath the hem of her dress. "Does that mean I get my massage now?"

"Sure," she said, fighting a grin.

Trent narrowed his eyes. "Why don't I believe you?"

"Because you know me too well?"

Trent tried to ignore the heat where their bodies met, but it was impossible. He wanted Josie now—no more playing around.

"Not as well as I'd like to know you," he blurted,

unsure exactly what he meant by that, except that he wanted to know every intimate detail of her body.

Josie's expression turned serious. "We shouldn't..."

When her voice trailed off, Trent leaned over and kissed her—a slow, coaxing kiss.

"I need lots of hands-on practice, teacher. Lots and lots," he said when he ended the kiss.

Josie's answer was a kiss of her own, passionate and deep. Their tongues danced in a prelude to what their bodies would do together as they fumbled to remove each other's clothing.

Her dress, with its thousand tiny buttons, proved too great a challenge for their urgent need, so Trent simply pushed it up to her waist and paused for a moment to admire her naked lower half. Breathless with desire, he slid the straps of her dress down over her shoulders to reveal her naked breasts—she'd gone braless, too—then leaned in to taste each one.

Josie slid his shirt from his shoulders and he shrugged it off, but there was no time to remove his slacks, not when she reached down and massaged his throbbing cock with her small, perfect hands. Trent forgot to breathe as she found all the right spots. Finally he had to nudge her hand away so he could take what he couldn't wait another moment for.

He found a condom in his wallet and, with shaking hands, he tugged it on in record time.

He grasped her hips and lifted her body up to meet his, then thrust into her with as much restraint as he could manage. She was slick and hot, ready for whatever he could give, so he tossed aside his restraint and began a fast, urgent rhythm.

Josie clung to him and met his thrusting with her

own. As they kissed, their moans and gasps mingled together, until they built up to a point of no return.

Their climax came fast and simultaneously, before Trent even had a chance to slow down and linger over their pleasure. Her release was as intense as his, judging by the way she cried out and convulsed against him.

He saw fireworks behind his eyelids, felt waves of pure ecstasy wash through his body, and sensed a tug of something deep inside his soul.

This just felt…right.

When they finally settled against each other to rest, Trent brushed aside a few strands of blond hair that had sprayed across Josie's eyes. He traced her jawline with his fingertips and pressed a soft kiss on her cheek.

Josie smiled a slow, peaceful smile. "That was intense."

Now wasn't the time to analyze the emotion that swelled in his chest. Not when they had all night to slow down and explore each other.

"Yeah, intense is a good word for it. How about we take this to the bedroom, maybe even get all the way undressed?"

Josie tossed a glance at the bag of carry-out, forgotten on a nearby table. "I was thinking we could head for the kitchen. I sort of worked up an appetite."

For the first time that evening, Trent noticed that he was hungry, too. He pushed himself off of Josie and stood, then helped her up from the couch. "I guess I can let you eat, if you have to. But I've got plans for you tonight, woman—"

She smiled as she tugged her dress back into place, depriving Trent of a glorious view of her perfect breasts. "Come on, Stud Boy. I know some interesting uses for pasta."

JOSIE LOOKED AROUND at the circle of faces in the seminar, many of which had grown more than just familiar to her in the past few months. These were people she knew intimately in an odd sort of way.

There was Sheila Beckley, who loved oral sex and whose husband found it an awful chore to perform that particular task. There was Miles MacGruder, who was overcoming a fear of vaginas, acquired when he discovered his previous wife had been cheating on him for years. How he and the current Mrs. MacGruder had managed to get together, what with his fear and all, was beyond Josie.

And there were Todd and Sandy West, who loved to have sex so much they came to the center for new ideas every week.

Together, the regulars at the Lovers for Life Center formed an odd sort of family, with Josie now at its center. Without intending to, she'd become the new Grande Dame. She'd taken her mother's place.

And for the most part she'd managed to be an utter and complete failure.

She was no closer to saving the center now than she had been when she'd first taken it over. Thinking about her imminent failure was getting her nowhere, so she tried to focus on the seminar discussion that had gotten away from her. Tonight's topic was "Living Fantasies: Revealing Your Innermost Desires To Your Mate."

"…hot wax on my nipples," Sandy West was saying.

Ouch.

"And the handcuffs? They stay on during sex?" her husband asked.

"Oh, yes."

That must have wrapped up Sandy's secret fantasy,

because everyone looked to Josie to guide the conversation onward. Except she'd spaced out so totally she had no idea what they were supposed to discuss next.

Josie glanced down at her notes. Thank goodness she'd placed a thumb where they had left off, and it was still there.

"Okay, now that we've heard from a few of the brave female spouses, how about we have a few volunteers from the husbands among us share your favorite fantasies?"

Todd West's hand shot up. No surprise there.

"Okay, Todd. Go ahead."

"We're in the woods," he began, and instantly Josie's thoughts turned to Trent.

What was it about men and wilderness sex fantasies? A relic from their caveman days, possibly? Josie felt her entire body heat up at the thought of the day Trent had described in such vivid detail his own favorite fantasy. Oh, how he'd reeled her in. Never once had she guessed his true motive.

Ever since her chat with Erika, Josie had been trying to wrap her mind around how she felt about Trent, about his possible motives, about everything. And now, especially about last night. So much for Erika's advice to stay out of bed.

Since she'd stopped focusing on trying to seduce Trent, the chemistry between them had been different. They'd felt like old friends, lovers, companions—all the things she imagined real couples feeling when they were truly, deeply happy. It had been perfectly natural for them to have sex. Josie had never experienced such a satisfying relationship with a man, but she'd always weakly held out the belief that they existed. Until now.

Now she was confused. What she and Trent had was

based on sex, nothing more. So, she kept reminding herself, it must have just been that her desperate libido was making a lot more of their relationship than was really there. Oh, but was she ever enjoying herself in the meantime.

And she realized with a start as she sat there among her students, she wanted the center to succeed almost as badly as she wanted Trent in her bed. Maybe more so, because where sex with Trent would surely be fleeting, the legacy of the center would live on for years to come.

The *legacy?* Where had that idea come from? In the space of a few months Josie had gone from carrying around an adolescent resentment for this place to thinking of it as a second home.

She was absolutely not going to let the Lovers for Life Center go out of business, no matter what she had to do.

She guided her way through the rest of the seminar, said all the right words to the students as they spoke to her on their way out, then headed straight for the door herself.

She drove to her mother's house, hoping Rafaela could offer a little guidance, or at least a little moral support. Besides, she'd sort of been missing her mother lately.

Not that she could ever tell her such a thing.

At her mother's condo, the lights were on and she could see someone moving around in the bedroom. Josie knocked, then let herself in with her personal key. She found her mother finally unpacking bags from her trip to Prague.

Rafaela's idea of unpacking was to open a drawer and dump the contents of the suitcase inside. Tonight, though, she was being extra organized. Josie sat on the bed and watched her mother fling dresses into the closet, cosmetics onto the dresser, slinky lingerie into a drawer. She must have been angry, because that was the only time she made any attempt to create order in her life.

"Why are you just now unpacking?" Josie crossed her legs on the bed and settled in to watch the show. Her mother's anger never failed to provide one.

"I just haven't felt like it until now, Josephine."

Her mother was the only person who called her by her full name. She said it was strong, the name of a woman with a backbone; that "Josie" was only a proper name for a milk cow.

"Are you going to tell me what's bothering you?"

Her mother continued to work without acknowledging the question.

Finally she said, "It's that Tony O'Reilly, actually. Trent's father."

Oh, right. Josie suppressed a smile. She should have known better than to try her hand at matchmaking.

"What did he do to upset you?"

"I don't want to talk about it."

Uh-oh. "That bad, huh?"

Rafaela halted her unpacking, a black lace bra dangling from her hand. "That man is infuriating."

Josie decided she'd better change the subject before her mother flew off the handle. "I have some new things going on at the center."

"That's nice, dear."

"Trent and I designed a weekend getaway for couples. It's sort of a wilderness experience, combined with sensuality seminars on site."

"Sounds like a good idea, although I'd prefer my adventures to take place in a hotel with room service."

"There's been a lot of interest so far. The trip is next weekend, and it's fully booked already."

Her mother began to rummage through her closet, rearranging things by color and type of clothing, a completely unheard-of practice in the Marcus household before today.

"I was hoping you might lead seminars once a week next month. It would draw in a lot of business."

"Sure, Josephine. I can do that," she said, sounding distracted.

"Mom, why don't you just tell me what you're so angry about? It'll make you feel better."

"Fine, you want to know what he said? That man made insinuations that I've had plastic surgery to stay young-looking! Can you believe that? Never in my life!" She clenched her fist tight, crushing a silk dress in the process.

"I'm sure he was just teasing. Maybe he meant it as a compliment. I wish you'd give him a second chance."

"Wish all you want, it doesn't matter. I'm quite sure he won't want to go on a date with me after what I said about his hairpiece."

"Mom! He doesn't wear a hairpiece."

"No? Well, you could have fooled me. He's got quite a head of hair for an old fogy then."

"Isn't he your age?"

She slammed her empty suitcase shut and hauled it off the bed. "Men age faster than women—it's a known fact."

TRENT HAD SPENT the week since their last lesson trying not to think too much about the feelings that had been stirred up during his little extra-credit project. It wasn't going to do him any good to daydream about having a real relationship with Josie until she showed some sign of being interested in one.

But now that they were here together again, he couldn't help feeling as if they were more than just casual lovers.

"Tonight's lesson begins with a pop quiz," Josie said, looking inordinately pleased with herself.

"Great."

She frowned at his sarcasm. "You don't like my quizzes?"

"When I asked for sex lessons, they weren't what I had in mind."

Trent jabbed a fork into his pasta, while Josie twirled fettuccine onto hers, seemingly unable to summon an appetite.

"First question. When does a woman like to begin foreplay?"

"Before sex?" He grinned when she shot him a warning glare.

"Okay, *when* before sex?"

"I don't get it. Are you looking for a time here, like ten o'clock?"

She shrugged. "Just whatever you think."

"A half hour before sex," he said, sure that if he wasn't right, he was close enough.

"No."

"No?"

"If you learn nothing else from me in the course of our lessons, learn this—a woman becomes aroused differently than a man."

He made a show of mouthing what she'd just said as if committing it to memory. "You're not going to educate me about the clitoris now, are you? Because I'm pretty familiar with it already.''

She blushed. "I've noticed."

"I bet you have."

"Let's not get cocky. You have plenty to learn."

"So what, then?"

"A woman's arousal begins in the mind. And it's not necessarily connected to physical sensations, although they do play a role."

"Okay, you like to think about sex before you have it."

"That isn't what I mean."

He gave her an I'm-listening look.

"The process of arousal for a woman is complex. It can begin with any affection, affirmation or positive interaction she has with her lover throughout the day. The more, the better. Especially if he goes out of his way to be solicitous, to behave like the Ideal Man."

"The Ideal Man? That's me, right?"

She suppressed a grin. "Ha, ha. We hope it will be by the end of these lessons."

"Aside from knowing his way around the clitoris, what qualities constitute the Ideal Man?" Trent asked, making a show of appearing eager to learn.

"He's truly interested in his lover, he cherishes her, he cares deeply about her thoughts and opinions..."

"And this has what to do with his being a stud in bed?"

"For a woman, it's all connected to how strongly she can respond to him sexually."

Josie sat back in her chair, watching him. She must have thought she could confuse him with all her pop psychology mumbo jumbo, but he'd heard it before.

"So the more devoted the guy, the stronger her orgasm is?"

"That's not what I'm saying."

"Can a woman have great sex without all this stuff you're talking about?"

She frowned. "Of course, but—"

"Then that's what I want to know. How to turn a woman on without all this extra out-of-bed stuff," he said, just to rile her for the fun of it.

"Aren't you interested in having a happy, committed relationship to go along with your great sex?"

"No," he lied.

"No?" she mumbled with her mouth full of fettuccine Alfredo.

"Okay, I'd be happy with either or both, but tonight I'm interested in the great sex part, and it's your job to teach me that."

"I can't in good conscience teach one without touching upon the other. They go hand in hand."

Trent raised an eyebrow. "What about the great sex you've had with me? You could hardly call what we have a happy and committed relationship. Or was it not as good for you as it was for me?"

Josie gave him a funny look and stabbed a noodle with her fork. "Of course we had great sex, and you have a point there, but our situation is pretty unique, wouldn't you say?"

"Yeah," he said, ready to skip over the subject entirely before he made a complete fool of himself.

"Why aren't you interested in the relationship aspects of my lesson?"

He blurted, "Why should you care? I've never known you to have any interest in serious relationships, either."

Josie opened her mouth to speak, then seemed to reconsider what she was about to say. "I'm not the student here—you are. I wouldn't be a good teacher if I didn't present the best information I know about sexuality."

She was getting annoyed with him. Trent tried to hide his smile, but she noticed.

"What's so amusing?"

"You've got a little something on your front tooth, that's all," he lied.

Josie wiped at her tooth with a napkin. "Still there?"

"Nope, you got it."

"Could we please get back to our lesson now?"

"Sure, you were about to tell me how to have great sex without all the commitment."

"No, I wasn't. You're the one having problems in the bedroom, remember?"

Ouch. She had him there, even if they were imaginary problems. He couldn't very well admit the truth now. "How could I forget?"

"And I'm the expert you turned to, so will you at least try it my way? That is, unless you have anything you need to *tell* me?"

Huh? Did she know more than she was letting on? "What's that supposed to mean?"

"Oh, nothing." She paused. "*Now* can we get back to the lesson?"

"Sure." He offered a conciliatory grin.

"Where were we... Oh, right, the Ideal Man. As I was saying, he's a man who understands how to give physical affection without it always leading to sex. I admit, you did a very nice job of that in your extra-credit project, but you don't even have to go to such lengths on an everyday basis. Just a simple back massage would do.''

''Sounds pretty easy.''

''You'd think so, but most men fail miserably in this arena.''

Trent finished the last of his dinner and downed a few gulps of beer.

Josie continued after a pause for effect. ''Men tend to become physically affectionate when they're ready for sex. Women need and want close physical contact as part of all their interactions.''

''How close?''

''It could be any physical contact, especially holding hands, touching her hair, kissing, hugging, little caresses for no apparent reason.''

''If I do all that, I'm gonna be ready for sex.''

''But see, that's the problem. Women need that kind of contact to not always be a direct prelude to intercourse.''

''So how will this make me a better lover?''

''Because when it is finally time for sex, the woman will come into the experience far more enthusiastically.''

''Ah. Interesting.'' Trent thought about how he normally interacted with his girlfriends. Did he do even half this stuff Josie was talking about?

Okay, so maybe he'd been lagging a bit in the Ideal Man department, but no one had left unsatisfied yet.

At least, not as far as he knew.

Oh, hell, what was he doing letting Josie's mumbo jumbo get to him like this?

''I think I've given you plenty to work on for now. I'd like to see you put these suggestions into practice.''

''You want me to be the Ideal Man for you?''

She shrugged and smiled. "Well, you can *try*."

"Will I be rewarded with a night of unforgettable hypothetical sex?"

"Hypothetically, anything could happen."

Yeah, didn't he know it.

Josie stood and took her plate to the sink, then rinsed it off and put it in the dishwasher.

"I thought we could do something mundane, to simulate everyday interactions between two lovers, so we'll go to the grocery store. I need to pick up some things, anyway."

"I'm supposed to make eyes at you and caress your hair over fresh produce?"

"That's entirely up to you."

"Hmm, how would the Ideal Man grocery shop, I wonder?"

Trent picked up a bottle of salad dressing from the table and made as though he was inspecting it for purchase. He went over to where Josie stood at the sink, grabbed her by the waist, and pulled her to him. Their bodies molded together in all the right places. He gazed into her eyes as if searching for the secrets of her heart.

"Look here, darling. This condiment is high in sodium. What do you think about that?"

Josie tried to appear annoyed, but a grin gave her away. "Could you at least try to be serious?"

He pulled her closer as she squirmed to get away. "Only if you promise to share with me all your most intimate thoughts about ranch dressing."

11

JOSIE ADMITTED to herself in the produce aisle that she might have made a grave mistake. She'd realized too late that taking one impossibly sexy man, telling him the secret to every woman's heart, and then asking him to try out his newly learned skills on her was a recipe for emotional disaster.

But everything would work out fine if she could just keep her heart out of it. That should be no problem as long as she reminded herself every thirty seconds or so that Trent was only acting, that he wasn't really interested in a relationship with her—or anyone else for that matter. He was still the same old wolf, nicely outfitted in a new sheep costume.

Trent slid his arm around her waist and pulled her close as she inspected an apple.

"One little bite won't hurt you," he said. "That snake over there just told me so."

"Isn't that supposed to be my line?"

She dropped the apple into a bag with the rest that had passed inspection. Without making a single comment on the wickedness of women leading men into temptation, Trent dutifully took the bag of apples from her and tied it, then put it in the cart.

"What's next on your list, dear?"

Wow, was he ever trying to pass tonight's test.

"Um…" Josie frowned, at a complete loss over what

she'd cook for dinner during the week. As usual, she had forgotten to make a list.

"I was thinking I could make dinner one night, whatever you want. Pick it out, and I'll cook it," Trent said.

If he kept on like this, Josie was going to have to strip him down and make love to him right next to the cantaloupes and honeydew melons.

"Don't make such a tempting offer unless you really mean it," she warned.

"I'm serious. Next lesson, we'll meet at your place and I'll cook."

"You know *how* to cook?"

Trent put a hand over his heart and staggered backward, as if wounded. "So little faith you have."

She shrugged. "Sorry, most guys I've dated knew how to cook meat on the grill, and that was it."

"How about my specialty, seafood lasagna?"

He still hadn't cracked a smile, but Josie couldn't get her brain to form a mental picture of Trent in the kitchen baking lasagna.

"That sounds great."

They moved through the aisles, Josie picking out items she regularly bought, plus a few dinners, and Trent selecting the ingredients for the meal he would make. She couldn't help but be intrigued by his selections. Real garlic, for instance. She couldn't even recall if she'd ever met a man who knew what to do with a clove of garlic.

When they reached the checkout, Trent separated the things he'd selected and paid for them himself, in spite of Josie's protest that she'd cover it since they were doing *her* grocery shopping.

At the car, he unloaded the cart into her trunk and then turned to Josie.

"How'd I do?" he asked.

"That depends on whether or not you're really going to make seafood lasagna for me."

"I wasn't acting tonight. I'm making dinner for you."

"Ah, so you really are the Ideal Man."

He grinned. "Your words, not mine."

"Do you know what the Ideal Man's lover does for him after he so valiantly helps her shop for groceries?" Josie asked.

"Rubs his feet?"

"No." She took a step forward and the distance between them shrunk to a matter of inches.

"I give up."

"She shows her gratitude in the way every man appreciates most, with physical affection."

Trent slid his hands around her waist. "This, I like."

His pelvis pressed into her and she felt him grow hard against her belly. Then he sat on the bumper of the car and pulled her between his legs, bringing his mouth to hers at the same time.

Josie kissed him with all she had.

Their kisses were no longer new and unfamiliar. They explored now, enjoyed a familiar heat, an easy rhythm that only came with familiarity. If she didn't know better, Josie would have thought she was kissing her one true love and not just a temporary lover.

"Mmm—" He pulled away. "Let's don't do this in a parking lot. I'm sure we can come up with someplace that has a little more atmosphere."

Let's don't do *this?* Did he mean what she hoped he meant? Josie's insides heated up at the prospect of making love to Trent again. Forget Erika Li and her silly rules. What Josie needed was sex with Trent, and lots of it.

A teenager pushing a long line of carts past them gawked openly, proving Trent's point.

"Not an exhibitionist, eh?" Josie whispered.

"Some things deserve the honor of privacy."

"Some things like what?"

He slid his hands down her waist to the curve of her rear end and squeezed. "Like this."

"But no one's looking now. Don't you like the thrill of possibly getting caught?"

He narrowed his eyes at her. "I'm not one of your kooky sex school rejects."

"My students are not rejects!"

"Okay, but they are kooky."

"Aren't you forgetting that *you* are one of my students now?"

"But I don't sit around in a circle with a bunch of other losers whining about sex problems."

"Ah, I see."

He pulled her closer. "I'm smart enough to talk the sexy instructor into giving me private, hands-on, one-on-one lessons."

JOSIE YAWNED and scanned her list of things to do before leaving on the weekend retreat. As far as she could tell, everything was done, but she was too exhausted to care much if she'd forgotten anything. The final details had been handled, the students had been registered, and today was the day they would head for the wilderness. For two days and three nights, Josie would be leading workshops in the woods, roughing it in a remote cabin, fighting off mosquitoes and Trent.

Ever since the last lesson she'd had with Trent two

weeks ago, she'd been avoiding him for reasons she couldn't explain and didn't want to think about. She'd canceled this week's lesson with the excuse that she was too busy working at the center—and that had been true. Pretty much.

She stared into her half-empty suitcase, wondering what on earth a woman was supposed to pack for a sensual adventure trip. More specifically, a sensual adventure trip on which she was the sensuality instructor.

When her doorbell rang she realized it was time for Trent to pick her up, and she wasn't even finished packing. She hurried to let him in. He stood in the doorway holding several bags.

"Hey, I brought your gear."

"Gear?" He didn't have a bicycle in one of those bags, did he?

"You can't go biking without the proper attire, the right shoes, a pair of padded gloves, and a helmet. I need you to check all this stuff out and tell me if it fits. I had to guess on the sizes, so I brought several of each."

"Oh, that kind of gear. Sorry, I'm running a little late. I'll just hurry and try these things on."

He nodded and took a seat on her couch.

Josie was at her bedroom door when she remembered her manners. "Thank you," she said, stopping in the doorway. "For bringing me these things. It was really thoughtful."

He shrugged. "No problem. There's also some sunblock and bug repellent in there."

Inside the bedroom, Josie dug into the bag and pulled out several garments. Very skimpy garments, in her estimation. Was this really what female mountain bikers wore these days, or was this Trent's idea of a joke?

There were a couple of brightly colored spandex tops that amounted to little more than sports bras, along with matching bike shorts short enough to qualify as hot pants. She dropped the outfits back into the bag and stormed out to the living room again.

"You're joking, right?"

Trent looked up innocently from last month's issue of *Cosmo,* which he'd found on her end table. "About what?"

"You don't really expect me to go trekking into the wilderness dressed like this." She held up the bag that advertised his business, Extreme Sports, in jagged black letters.

"What's wrong with those outfits?" he asked. But she could see by the barely repressed smile that he was baiting her.

"I'm not even remotely toned enough to go out in public in this much spandex."

"Believe me, you're toned enough. I picked those out specifically with your, uh, figure in mind." The corner of his mouth twitched, and Josie had a nearly uncontrollable urge to climb onto his lap and kiss him senseless.

First she would kiss him, then she'd strangle him.

"I bet you did," she said. "I'm not wearing these."

"Those clothes make perfect sense for the sport. It's going to be hot, and if you feel self-conscious, don't worry, we'll hardly see anyone else. The people we do see will be busy navigating the trails, not evaluating your fashion statement."

"Why can't I just wear a T-shirt and some regular shorts?"

"You can if you want. The shorts I brought just have a little extra padding in the seat for comfort, and the fabric of the outfits is a special microfiber that keeps moisture away from your skin.''

Okay, so the outfits didn't sound so scandalous when he put it that way. ''And I don't suppose these special fabrics come in a loose-fitting variety.''

''Sure they do. I just wanted to see you in tight clothes, that's all.''

If he really thought she'd look sexy in the bike outfits, then maybe it would be a good idea to wear them. But then she pictured her rear end clad in padded spandex shorts and she shuddered. She'd just have to stay seated on her bike as much as possible. And never let Trent walk behind her. She'd also have to constantly think about sucking in her belly, so it would be just like being naked. Great, she was going on a naked biking trip.

She hurriedly packed her bag and loaded it in Trent's SUV parked outside her apartment. They had made a van available for students who didn't want to drive to Lake Tahoe, but for themselves, Trent insisted that he would drive and Josie could ride with him.

Josie had spent the past two weeks working night and day at the center, making one last-ditch effort to save it from bankruptcy. Her mother had wandered in to help on occasion, and Erika had done a fabulous job keeping the place running smoothly for the customers, but still, Josie was exhausted. What she needed was a real long-weekend vacation, not a working one.

Trent tried to talk to her during the ride, but she dozed off as they were driving through Oakland, and didn't wake up until they'd pulled in to the state park.

Josie yawned and stretched, momentarily bewildered to find herself alone in a strange vehicle. They were parked in the shade of a grove of trees, next to a rustic, wood building. Moments later Trent came walking out of the building and smiled at her.

He opened her door and offered his hand for her to climb out. "You crashed hard. Back around Sacramento, I thought you were just being a really good listener until you started snoring."

She wrinkled up her brow. "I snored?"

"You drooled a little, too. I just got us registered, but there was a booking mix-up. They put us in separate cabins."

Josie felt a little twinge of giddiness that Trent had even assumed they'd be sharing a cabin. "I'm sure they could still put us in the same cabin. That is, if we want to share one."

Trent gave Josie a once-over. "You and I both need our rest, and I have a feeling that if we're in a cabin together, one thing we *won't* be doing is resting."

Josie stifled a yawn. A good night's rest sounded so heavenly right now. After weeks of working night and day at the center, she couldn't argue with his logic.

"Well, if you don't mind sleeping alone..."

"Really it's for my own good as much as yours. I need all the physical strength I can get to lead a weekend full of tours." He smiled sheepishly.

Josie shrugged her acceptance. A bed, empty or not, was all she wanted now.

"We can leave the truck and the luggage here and walk to the cabins. It's a short walk through the woods. Someone will bring our luggage on an electric car."

Rubbing her eyes and blinking in the shaded sunlight, Josie followed Trent as they made their way along a paved trail.

A few minutes later they came to a small cabin. "Here we are."

"Is this my cabin or yours?"

"Yours. Mine's supposed to be a couple of minutes farther down the path." He pulled a key out of his pocket and handed it to her.

Josie took the key and fumbled to get the door open. Once she'd succeeded, she turned to Trent. "I'm not sure how I'll manage to stay awake to greet my students as they arrive."

He gave her a sympathetic look. "Why don't you stay here and get some more rest? Just tell me what I need to do for everyone this evening."

She recalled mumbling some instructions before she let herself into the cabin and fell into bed.

What must have been hours later, she sat up in bed to find that it was light outside, but it looked more like bright morning light than what she'd fallen asleep to.

The clock on the nightstand confirmed that it was eight-thirty in the morning. Uh-oh. She had a seminar starting in a half hour, and she didn't even know her way around the campgrounds yet.

Someone knocked at the door and Josie shuffled out of bed to answer. She noticed on the way that the cabin was a pretty well-equipped one, complete with a cozy fireplace sitting area and a kitchenette.

Trent was at the door. "Morning, Sleeping Beauty. I brought coffee," he said, holding up a thermos.

"Thank you. I can't believe how long I slept. I have a seminar at nine, and I'm not even prepared."

"Sorry, I would have woken you if I'd known."

She looked down to see that she was still wearing her jeans and top from the day before. Yikes. "It's okay, I just have to hurry, get cleaned up and dressed, if you don't mind." Josie spotted the bathroom and hurried to it. A few minutes later, as she was brushing her teeth, Trent knocked and poked his head inside.

"I put the coffee on the table. We'll meet up tonight, after I finish leading the evening hike?"

Josie rinsed her mouth out. "I have a late-night seminar tonight. 'Keeping the Marriage Fire Burning.' You're welcome to attend."

He raised an eyebrow. "Sounds riveting. I'll see you later."

She watched as he turned and left the doorway, his wide shoulders sagging a little. It surprised her to realize that he was disappointed that they couldn't spend time together.

Trent? Wanting more of her time? Wow. She thought back to Erika's advice. Was he just looking for more opportunities for vengeance or was he longing for something more? Was it just sex, or could it be possible that Trent the Playboy wanted a real relationship?

Josie didn't want to consider the possibilities. She had work to focus on. She just wanted to keep things simple with Trent. And most of all, she didn't want to start analyzing her own conflicted feelings.

Some hornet's nests were better left undisturbed.

TRENT SWATTED at a mosquito on his arm, then glanced at his watch. It was seven-thirty, time for all the over-sexed seminar attendees to be here in the pavilion, not off scaring the wild animals somewhere. But so far only a few couples had appeared.

Josie glanced up from some papers she was flipping through and flashed Trent a weak smile. She knew he wasn't happy to be playing her assistant again. He'd only agreed to it after getting her solemn word that no tools of torture or restraint would be involved. Not that he'd mind being restrained by her, or even tortured a little bit, but *not* in front of an audience.

So far this weekend had been too busy for them to really spend any time together. With the two of them being responsible for making sure the entire trip ran smoothly for everyone, all the while performing their official teaching and tour guide duties, they'd done little more than pass each other on the way to one place or another. Josie's request for his help had come only an hour ago over dinner.

Trent tried to keep his disappointment in check. He couldn't expect anything from her. Not three years ago, and not now.

Several more couples arrived by way of a path through the nearby woods, and Trent realized that Josie still hadn't told him what exactly the seminar topic would be. She'd simply revealed the rather cryptic title, which was also written on a dry-erase board a few feet away. Love Talk.

It sounded benign enough, but now he realized its vagueness could mean trouble. He got up from his seat at a picnic table and went to Josie. She glanced up from her notes again and blinked at the setting sun that peaked through the trees.

"What exactly does 'Love Talk' mean?" he asked.

"Oh, I almost forgot. I have a little script here for you to go by during the seminar."

Trent took the piece of paper she handed him and frowned at it. His first line was, "I'm feeling unsatisfied with the lack of oral sex in our lovemaking."

Huh? "You didn't answer my question."

"We'll be discussing ways to have clear and loving communication about sexual issues in marriage. I'll need you to help me model appropriate ways to discuss sex issues.''

Oh, yippee. "Couldn't you just have one of the couples in the seminar do this modeling stuff?''

"This is a topic that will help you with your own love life, so I want *you* to do it.'' She smiled sweetly. "Please.''

"Well, since you said 'please'...''

Josie checked her watch. "We'd better get started.'' She turned to the group of seven couples that had gathered at several picnic tables in the pavilion. "Are you ready to revolutionize your sex lives?''

Half the attendees responded with enthusiastic whoops and hollers, while the other half nodded to affirm their readiness for a sexual revolution.

"One of the greatest hindrances to a satisfying sex life, even within marriage, is lack of communication. We're afraid to ask for what we want, afraid to be specific, and unsure how or when to broach the subject.''

Hmm, another wild idea was forming in Trent's head. He and Josie had been suffering from their own lack of communication. Maybe this was his chance to set things straight between them. Either that or get her really, really mad.

He looked down at his script again, at the lines Josie wanted him to repeat.

Josie continued. "I'd like you to listen as my assistant and I engage in a conversation about our hypothetical married sex life, and as you listen, take note of what you think goes right—and wrong—in the conversation.''

She pulled up a chair next to Trent and read from a script of her own. "Honey, is something wrong? You've been acting distant lately.''

Trent glanced at his oral sex line, and then made up a line of his own. "Yeah, something's wrong. You've been using me for sex, haven't you?"

Josie stared at him, her jaw sagging. "W-what?" She leaned in and whispered, "That's not on the script!"

He ignored her and continued. "Sex, sex, sex. All you ever want from me is sex. I'm tired of being your pleasure toy!"

She blushed an explosive shade of red. This was turning out to be fun, after all.

"Would you please follow the script?" she said through clenched teeth.

"I have needs, too, you know. I'm not just a sex machine."

Their audience was clearly enjoying the show, judging by their undivided attention on the unfolding skit.

"Y-you're the one who wanted sex lessons!" she blurted, then realized her error. Josie turned to the class. "I'm sorry, my assistant is being a bit uncooperative."

"I demand emotional satisfaction!" he said in his best indignant female voice, trying hard not to laugh.

"You can go now. I'll do this seminar without you."

Trent held up his hands in surrender. "Hey, I'm sorry. I was just having a little fun."

"Go!" she said, but he could tell she didn't really mean it.

"Aw, come on, let him stay!" someone in the audience called out. "We want to hear more about those sex lessons."

Trent grinned. "I'll follow the script now, I promise."

"One more deviation and you're out of here. Understand?"

Okay, so maybe he'd chosen a cowardly way to

broach the subject of their relationship. Maybe it was time for him to get serious about Josie, if she could prove she was finished with running away.

SO FAR, the Lovers for Life Center's first-ever Sensual Adventure Retreat was a success. Attendees had been approaching Josie all weekend to thank her for sponsoring it or to express their interest in going on another. She'd already decided to offer retreats on a regular basis, maybe even once a season, if she managed to make the center profitable again.

Josie walked along the path that led from the cabins to the pavilion. Today was the last day of the retreat. She didn't have any more seminars scheduled and she was eager to spend some time with Trent. They'd hardly gotten a moment alone together all weekend, with his leading adventure excursions and her leading seminars.

But today she'd set aside the afternoon to go on the bike ride he'd requested. He had a morning bike tour that was supposed to be wrapping up now, and then he'd take her out for their ride alone together.

Although she and wheeled vehicles didn't get along, she was looking forward to the day. For an afternoon alone with Trent, she'd happily endure a few bumps and bruises.

There was still an odd tension between them, something she couldn't name, but she figured it would work itself out in a day of relaxing together. She'd come to see Trent as a friend in the past two months—a fact that still sometimes amazed her—even with his embarrassing little performance yesterday at the seminar.

She wasn't sure what all that had been about, but knowing Trent, she'd written it off as his sense of humor getting a little out of control. He did love baiting her, after all.

He'd always stood as a sort of mythical figure in her past, someone untouchable, and now she'd touched him in just about every way imaginable. Somehow, in the midst of all their flirting and foreplay and lovemaking, they'd become friends.

Friends who were also lovers. So what was the name for that? Certainly they didn't have a real romantic relationship. Theirs had been a student-teacher arrangement, nothing more. Trent was incapable of maintaining a long, meaningful relationship, and Josie was uninterested in one.

She spotted Trent up ahead in the pavilion, and she waved to him. He had two bikes there waiting for them.

After he'd given her a few pointers, they were off on what Trent called "a fairly easy trail."

Josie firmly believed that if humans had been meant to ride around on two wheels, they would have been born with wheels instead of legs. She hated riding bikes, and she especially hated riding bikes on muddy paths near trees that she might at any moment crash into.

"Keep your eyes focused ahead on the trail, not down at your feet," Trent instructed from behind on his own mountain bike.

"It's these feet-holder things. They're uncomfortable."

"Just ignore them and keep going. You'll get used to the sensation after a while."

Sure. Right after she got used to having a skinny bike seat jammed up her rear. She had an intense fear that she was going to develop blisters in the most painful place imaginable after a day on this godforsaken contraption.

"My hands hurt now. Can't we stop and rest?"

"Your hands will get used to it, too. Stop complaining. Our next break is in an hour."

Josie rolled her eyes. Take Trent away from the city and suddenly he was Survival Man, determined to whip everyone he encountered into tip-top shape so they could ride bikes around the woods for days at a time if they wanted. She couldn't imagine why anyone would want to do such a thing. The wilderness was nice and all, but that's what the Discovery Channel was for. No ugly bugs to encounter in person. No mud to get one's foot stuck in. No trees to crash into.

Okay, so there were trees in the city, and so she had once crashed her car into one. But it had been a minor crash, and a small tree, and Trent certainly didn't need to know about it.

But she had to admit, following Trent around the woods on a bike wasn't the worst way to spend a day. And maybe she was enjoying the mountain biking a tiny bit during those occasional moments when she was able to forget about all her discomforts.

Up ahead Josie saw a clearing and she wondered if faking a crash might buy them a few hours' rest in the nice, sunny field. She didn't have long to wonder, though, and she didn't have to worry about faking it, because the front wheel of her bike hit a tree stump. Suddenly Josie was sailing through the air, experiencing both sheer terror and that wonderful sense of free fall that comes in the moment before hitting the ground.

She landed in a patch of mud on the trail, which had the advantage of cushioning her fall and the disadvantage of being, well, mud. When she tried to right herself, her palms slipped in the ooze and she wound up going down face first.

"Josie, don't move. Let me check you out. Are you hurt anywhere?"

She would have answered except she had a mouth full of mud.

Strong hands grasped her, tested her legs, her arms, then pulled her up from the brown muck. She spit and hacked and spit some more, until most of the gritty substance was gone from her mouth.

"I think I'm okay."

Trent eased her down onto a dry grassy area and kneeled next to her, worry creasing his brow. "Nothing hurts?"

This was her chance to get a break from bike riding, so she jumped at it. "Well, I don't know. I think I hit my knee. It's starting to feel a little stiff. Maybe we could rest awhile and make sure it's okay."

"Sounds good. I'm getting hungry for lunch anyway. There are some wet wipes in my backpack, but I'm pretty sure there aren't enough to get you cleaned up."

"What about the water bottle? I could use that."

He shook his head. "We need it to drink. One of the first rules of wilderness survival—never waste your water."

"I can't just go around coated in mud all day."

"We passed a creek a little ways back. I think it runs along this way." He pointed toward the clearing. "Think you can walk a bit?"

She debated how much of an act she should put on. Being injured might come in handy later in avoiding further bike rides. And it might be fun to have Trent play nurse to her for a while.

"Let's see." She extended a hand for him to help her up, but once she stood, she winced in pain at her pretend-gimp knee.

"Too painful to walk?"

"No, no. I'll be fine, but maybe some support would help."

Trent slid his arm around her waist and she leaned into him, suddenly seeing all sorts of possible advantages to being injured. The close contact made her forget how miserable she'd felt a moment ago, and her mind occupied itself with fantasies about what might happen out here between the two of them, all alone.

Maybe getting close to nature wasn't such a bad deal, after all.

12

TRENT FELT LIKE A JERK. He never should have taken someone as awkward on a bike as Josie on an intermediate trail so soon. He'd just assumed since she was young and fit that she could handle it. He hadn't counted on her being bicycle-impaired.

And now he wondered how they'd make it back to the campground if her knee was seriously hurt, though it didn't look bad. No swelling, no intense pain. Yet she was limping around pretty badly and as they made their way to the creek, she put quite a bit of her weight on him.

Not that he minded. Even covered in mud, she had the power to turn his mind to mush, and he had a hard time focusing on the fact that she was injured when her body was pressed against his. He could think of a dozen ways off the top of his head to make her forget about her knee, but he doubted she'd be in the mood for any of them after sailing headfirst over her bike the way she just had.

Josie cast a glance over her shoulder. "Are you sure our bikes will be safe back there?"

"Positive. No one will even be able to see them hidden under that bush, so stop worrying. We're almost there. You doing okay?"

"Yep, fine. Sorry I'm getting you all muddy, too."

"Maybe we'll just have to take a bath together."

"Aren't there snakes and leeches and things in the creeks out here?"

"Have you ever even been out of the city before today?"

"Sure, we went to Calistoga when I was a kid."

"I mean, really out of the city. To a farm or to go camping?"

"Does my mother strike you as the type to take her daughter on nature encounters?"

He chuckled. "No, definitely not."

"I did go to camp one summer, when I was eleven. I hated every minute of it, and I was nearly eaten alive by mosquitoes. Mother Nature and I are not on speaking terms."

"You just haven't had the right nature guide."

"Oh, yeah? What sorts of things could the right nature guide do for me?"

Oh, lots of things. Lots of bad, bad things. "Guess you'll just have to see for yourself."

Up ahead Trent spotted the glittering water of the creek, and then they could hear it, too. As light as she was, hauling Josie through the woods had still managed to get him sweaty and thirsty, so the water was a welcome sight.

When they reached the creek's edge, Josie knelt next to it and peered down as if inspecting its contents.

"The critters generally stay hidden when you come stomping up like we just did."

"So there *are* critters."

"Yeah, but I don't think you have anything to worry about. This water's all of four feet deep at its deepest point. You can see clear to the bottom."

She jumped back. "What are those things swimming around?"

He looked down to see that the source of her alarm was a fierce school of tadpoles. "Those? They're deadly baby water moccasins, but don't worry, they usually don't bite unless provoked."

"Ha, ha, very funny."

"Really, I lost a toe to one of them a few years back."

She smiled, and Trent noticed she was resting her weight equally on both legs.

"How's the knee?"

Her grin grew wider. "Oh, that? All better."

"Were you faking?"

"Never!"

"You were, too. I bet you just got tired of riding bikes." Trent took off his helmet and tossed it onto the shore.

"Well, you're a bit of a tyrant for a beginner like me."

"Sorry, I'll go easier on the trip back. I promise. We'd better get you cleaned up, though, before the mud dries."

Josie eyed the water again with suspicion.

"Such a city girl," Trent teased, shaking his head as he stripped off his shoes and socks.

A minute later he'd rid himself of his clothes and was wading in, the water lapping at his shins. "Come on, your turn."

But when he turned back to her, he saw that her expression had changed. She looked as if she were just now seeing the creek and its surroundings for the first time.

And then he realized, she was probably thinking of his fantasy. Him, her and a creek in the woods. Only she didn't know she was the star of that particular movie.

His whole body went on sexual alert as he realized this was his chance to act out that fantasy. Right here, once and for all. Chances like this were rare indeed.

"Remember that fantasy I told you about?" he asked.

She was taking off her mud-caked helmet now. Then she bent and removed her shoes and socks. Moments later he watched as she slipped out of her entire bike outfit, and stood on the shore naked. Waiting for him.

"I remember. Every detail."

Trent forgot how to breathe. When he finally recovered, she was wading out to him, splashing the remaining mud off of herself as she went. She bent and splashed her face in the water.

He reached out and wiped a streak of mud from her nose. As she stood only a few inches away, naked, wet and willing, he told her, "You are the woman in the fantasy, you know. It's you every time."

She smiled, then splashed him. Trent wiped the water from his eyes and laughed as Josie began to back up, retreating. "I'm not sure we can really stick to the specifics of your fantasy. I don't see any vines around here."

She was referring to the vine in Trent's creek fantasy that she'd use to tie him to the tree.

"That's okay, I have another wilderness-watering-hole fantasy."

"Oh?" She stopped her retreat, her perfect chest heaving from the exertion.

Not really, but hey, this could be fun. He improvised. "We're out in the woods together biking, and it's really hot, so we stop by the creek to cool off."

"Then we get undressed," Josie added.

Trent took a step, and then another step, closing the distance between them. "And we take turns rubbing the cool water over each other's bodies."

He cupped his hand and dipped it into the water, then brought it up and let the liquid drip down over her breasts. Her erect nipples contracted even more, and Trent let his thumb brush one of them, then trace the underside of her breast.

Josie reached up and let her wet hands glide over his shoulders, his arms, his chest. Then she reached behind him and splashed water onto his back, letting her breasts brush his abdomen. His whole body strained to possess her, but this was too much fun to rush.

"And then what happens?" she asked as Trent ran his hands over her silky skin, taking time to appreciate how sumptuous Josie looked wet.

"We spread out our clothes on the bank and lie in the sun to dry off."

Josie arched one eyebrow. "All we do is lie there and dry off?"

"You'll just have to wait and see," he said, lifting her into his arms and making his way toward the bank of the creek.

He set Josie back on her feet next to his pile of clothes, then arranged his garments and hers into a makeshift blanket as best he could. He kneeled and pulled Josie down beside him, then pressed her to the ground with his body.

"Then I do what I've been dying to do all weekend."

Josie gasped as his mouth claimed one of her damp breasts then the other. He trailed kisses over her chest and abdomen, watching gooseflesh appear wherever he kissed, savoring the sweet torture of wanting her so badly and not taking her.

"What exactly have you been dying to do?" she finally whispered in a tight voice.

"This," he said just before spreading her legs wide, lowering his mouth between her thighs and plunging his tongue into her.

She was already swollen with desire for him, slick and ready for lovemaking, but the taste of her was just too sweet to pass up. Josie bucked against his tongue, squirming as he explored her, teased her, branded her as his own.

When he couldn't wait another minute, Trent stopped. "And now we do what men and women have been doing in the woods together since the beginning of time."

She sat up on her elbows and gave him a speculative look. "Not so fast."

"What's wrong?"

"I've got a few wilderness fantasies of my own, you know."

She pushed Trent down onto the clothing and slid her hands over his chest and belly, torturously slow. She eventually trailed her fingers down to his cock, then stroked it with a feather touch. Just when he didn't think he could take another second of sweet torture—when he was about to pounce on her—she dipped her head and took him into her mouth.

Trent stifled a loud moan, aware on some level that they were out in the open, where anyone might hear. And that thought only increased the thrill.

Josie coaxed him just to the edge of orgasm, then stopped. Brought him to the edge again, then stopped again. The third time, he grasped the back of her head and in a weak voice that came out as more of a croak, begged her to quit.

She looked up at him, her eyes sparkling with pure mischief. It took all his willpower not to mount her right then.

Instead he dug into the pocket of his shorts on the ground beneath them for a condom, then put it on. Having felt how hard and uncomfortable the ground was to lie on, he decided they'd imitate the animals, since they were out in the wild anyway. He turned Josie around and guided her hips against him to enter her from behind.

His cock slid into her as if it were going home, as if their bodies had known each other for years, not just weeks. As it always should have been.

And they moved together so naturally, Trent wished it wouldn't have to end. Nothing had felt this right before, this easy, this perfect.

When they came, her climax following his by seconds, it seemed as if the entire wilderness had paused. Trent heard no birds or insects, nothing but the sound of their quickened breaths.

He pulled Josie up against him and showered her shoulder and neck in kisses as he wrapped his arms around her waist. If they could only stay this way…

A breeze picked up and cooled their fevered skin, and it seemed that the wilderness came to life again. A few nearby birds chirped. A cricket sang in the grass. As they remained locked in that intimate embrace, Trent held Josie tight and let his fantasy take over again. In the fantasy, she was his, now and forever.

JOSIE RETURNED from the weekend trip feeling as though she needed a retreat to recover from her retreat. Thanks to the biking trip, she ached from head to toe.

She'd come home to find a message on her answering

machine from the local counseling center to which she'd sent her résumé months ago. They had an opening for a marriage counselor and were interested in her for the job.

So here she sat in the lobby of Family Counseling Associates dressed in the navy suit she always wore to interviews. She scanned her résumé out of nervousness, glanced over at the oblivious receptionist across the room, smoothed her wool skirt over her legs, stilled her bobbing foot, wiped the dampness from her palms, and wondered for the hundredth time if she was making a mistake.

She should have been thrilled. It was the perfect opportunity, with perfect timing. The center still wasn't completely financially stable, and Josie was at her wit's end trying to save it. This job could be her way out. But whenever she thought of escaping the center, it felt more like she was abandoning it.

Sure, she'd come to enjoy the people there, even the work, but... But what?

Her thoughts kept circling back to Trent. Their afternoon together at the creek in the woods had been amazing. She still had trouble believing that *she* was the woman in his fantasy.

Maybe he'd said it to make her feel good...but no, there was something in the way they'd come together, something reverential about their lovemaking. She believed him.

But he was still the same Trent as before, and she was still the same Josie. Being good together in a physical sense didn't mean they could have a real relationship. She'd seen plenty of marriages fall apart when couples got married and discovered they had nothing in common except great sex. Josie didn't plan to make that mistake.

Confused about her feelings, Josie had called Trent a day after they'd gotten back to the city and told him she needed to reschedule their last lesson for a later date. She wanted to make sure she went into their final session with no illusions. Theirs was a business relationship that would be coming to an end—not a complicated romantic entanglement that she should feel any need to hang on to.

"Ms. Marcus?" a woman called from a nearby doorway.

Josie looked up to meet the smile of a matronly woman with steel-gray hair and a well-tailored pantsuit. When she reached the woman's side, they shook hands and Josie felt instantly at ease.

"I'm Eleanor Griffith. I hope you're not nervous. We're quite impressed with your credentials, and we've already gotten great references for you, so this interview is really just to see how our personalities mesh."

Josie kept her surprise in check. "Oh, that's good to hear."

She followed Eleanor into a comfortably decorated office and took a seat on a couch where the woman indicated for her to sit.

"We have five other counselors here at this center, all specializing in various areas of family counseling. I primarily work with children, and you would be one of two marriage counselors."

Josie nodded. She tried to focus as the woman went on about the work environment and the job, but her mind wandered back to Trent. Would he care if she took a job here? If she left the center and severed that final tie to him?

It was a question she shouldn't have desired the answer to so badly. She had let her ego get too involved in their lessons. To correct the problem, she would simply force herself to face their final session together as a professional task to which she owed her best work.

Trent had to be a client to her, nothing more. If she could remember that, she could enjoy their last night together for all it was worth.

As Eleanor Griffith discussed their philosophy, Josie found herself thinking about the center again. How could she leave now, when Erika was just getting started in her new role there, when the sensual adventure retreats were just getting started, when all the changes she'd made might possibly create a new momentum that would take the business in the right direction? How could she leave when the work there had become the focus of her life? She didn't know, but she had a feeling that if she didn't leave soon, she never would.

TRENT WASN'T SURE what he would miss more, Josie or their sex lessons. Part of him wanted to ask her to keep coming back every week, as his lover and friend, not as his instructor. But his common sense told him that with the way Josie had been avoiding him lately, she wasn't ready for any kind of commitment.

"Tonight we'll be having your final exam," she said, standing in his living room, possibly for the last time.

Trent smiled. "Will it be oral or written?"

"We'll start with a little oral, then move on to a hands-on skills demonstration."

"I bet you don't mean oral the way I'm hoping."

She laughed. "Would you stop!"

"Okay, okay, seriously. Let's begin, Madame Instructor."

Josie pulled out a chair at the dining room table and sat, motioning for him to do the same. She took out a pad of paper and began reading notes to herself. After a few moments she looked up at him and smiled.

"First exam question. Is it socially acceptable to con someone you know into giving you sex lessons you don't need as part of an elaborate revenge plot against that person?"

Ouch.

"When did you figure it out?"

Josie shrugged. "That's not important."

"Aw, come on. Did I give myself away somehow?"

"Not exactly," she said, and he got the message that she wouldn't discuss it any more. Women's intuition never failed to amaze him.

"I apologize for deceiving you."

"It's okay. I had fun, you had fun, no one got hurt."

That's exactly the attitude he'd hoped she would have in the end. Then why did it leave an empty feeling in his gut?

"I was going to tell you, but then I sort of gave up on the revenge thing the first time we had sex."

"So you really thought you could hold out on me for two months?" she asked, incredulous.

"I figured it would be fun trying, and fun if I failed, too."

"And here I thought for a while that I was just a really great instructor, then come to find out you didn't need me at all."

"That's not true." He grinned, feeling sheepish to admit, "I've actually learned a lot from our lessons. I hadn't intended to."

Josie smiled. "Thanks for saying that. How about you show me what you've learned now?"

He reached across the table for her hand, then led her to the bedroom. If this was truly their last night together, he wanted it to be special.

Trent undressed Josie slowly, savoring the feel of her skin, the curves of her body. She did the same for him.

Like two blind people seeing with their hands, remembering with their fingertips, they touched and touched some more. He never wanted to forget the feel of her. He wanted to savor every little inch.

His fingers dipped inside her hot flesh, teasing in and out until she squirmed and her breath quickened. He used his thumb to massage her clitoris at the same time, and he dipped his head to nip at her neck with his teeth. She clung to him and moaned into his ear as she grew wetter and wetter. She was ready for him, but if this was their last night together, he wanted to create memories that they wouldn't soon forget.

Trent leaned back on the bed and tugged her on top of him, then nudged her hips until she straddled his torso, then his shoulders. She held on to the headboard as he pleasured her with his tongue. He tasted her very essence and plunged inside.

He slid his hand up her rib cage to her breasts and toyed with her nipples, while Josie began to move with the rhythm of his tongue. Moments later she came, then collapsed beside him, gasping and quivering.

As he pulled her against him and pressed his mouth to her shoulder, he took note of how perfectly they fit together. Their bodies were made for each other, made for pleasuring and comforting and playing together. Tonight, if no other night, he wanted to make her see that, too.

He reached for the condom on his nightstand and slid it on.

"I want you inside me," she whispered, as if he needed any coaxing.

Trent's body trembled as he pressed himself against Josie from behind. As they lay there spooned together, he pulled her tighter against him and slid inside her. His erection met the hot dampness at her core and he closed his eyes. He saw stars in those first few moments of exquisite stillness, and then when he began to move, the stars burst.

Her tight, wet opening accommodated him just as perfectly as the rest of her body did. For the first time he understood the phrase "one flesh." They were of one flesh in those sweet, perfect moments of slow love-making. He cupped her breast in his hand and imagined that he was making love to his wife.

Josie arched her back, pressed her buttocks more firmly against him, and urged his cock deeper inside her. That simple shift of position set Trent on fire. He pulled away and rolled her onto her back, then positioned himself on top. He wanted to see her face when she came again.

Her legs parted for him and snaked around his hips, locking him in place. He kissed her as he plunged in deep, filling her, and she gasped into his mouth. Her kiss turned hungrier and greedier, while Trent's own need filled his chest and threatened to cut off his breath. During all these years of lusting after Josie, his fantasies of making love to her were nowhere near as good as the real thing. His feeble imagination couldn't have begun to reproduce the sweet, wet, intense mating they were engaged in now.

She plunged her fingers through his hair, down his

back, over his shoulders, as he worked them both up to the edge of climax, then backed off. Josie let out a frustrated growl, but he put a finger to her lips and smiled to reassure her that this wouldn't be like some of the previous nights.

"I want you," she whispered.

Still inside her, he rolled her on top of him and then pulled her to a sitting position. She tossed her head back and immediately began a rhythm of her own, rocking her hips as he stroked her breasts, her smooth belly, her round hips.

He tried to focus completely on the divine physical sensations, but the need in his chest kept growing. And then he realized it wasn't need at all, but rather an emotion he dared not name.

Trent massaged her breasts and tried with all his might to think about nothing but the soft weight of them in his hands. But the emotion was too strong. He had to face it.

Love.

There it was, plain as day, mocking his ridiculous plan for revenge. After all these years, he had to admit he loved Josie Marcus, Josie the Tease.

She bent and kissed his neck, his jaw, then his mouth, all the while moving him closer to the edge.

"I love you," he whispered when she came up for air, before he realized he was speaking the words out loud.

She froze for a split second, then continued moving her hips against him. "I love this, too."

This? Had she misunderstood him? Or was she pretending to misunderstand?

Oh, hell, he shouldn't have blurted something so stupid anyway. Not when he was half out of his mind with desire.

She quickened the pace and Trent's entire body tensed. His release came fast and hard, just as her muscles began to contract around him. Her gasps mingled with his own, and then she collapsed on top of him. Her blond curls tickled his face, but he was too spent to push them away.

Trent inhaled the sweet scent of Josie, and he knew in that moment that she was exactly the person he wanted to go to bed with every night, and to wake up with every morning, for the rest of his life.

If only she felt the same way.

JOSIE CAME into the kitchen dressed in her slightly rumpled outfit from the day before. It was the first time they'd spent the entire night together, after making love into the wee hours of the morning.

She yawned as she sat across from Trent at the table. With her hair tumbling over half her face, and her eyes still puffy from sleep, she looked like the woman he'd always imagined waking up with. They'd eat breakfast in bed on Saturday mornings, lie around reading the paper together, then make love.

Or maybe they'd skip the first two and get right down to business. That's what he would have loved to be doing with Josie at that moment, but she still thought theirs was a student-teacher relationship.

Maybe it was time to tell her the truth, that he was in love with her.

Josie poured herself a cup of coffee from the pot on the table. Pressing her hands against the outside of the hot mug, she shook her head. "How did humans survive before the invention of coffee?"

Trent smiled. "Early morning sex has a similar stimulating effect. Maybe that was their secret."

She took a sip and moaned a little more theatrically than the coffee called for.

"What's on your schedule today?" he asked, hoping she'd have time to hang out and talk.

"I have to meet my mother in a couple of hours to go over center business. She's going to help me with class schedules, that kind of thing."

"Has business improved at all?"

"It has," she said before taking a sip of coffee. "I've actually got the money to pay the rent this month, I think. Along with all the other bills."

"That's great."

She seemed to be focused on something else, though. "I still don't get it. If my mother is thinking of closing down the center unless I want to run it, then why did she make it so hard on me? Why did she take all the money, leave the place in near ruin, and expect me to somehow make it a profitable business again?"

Trent had wondered that himself. But Rafaela always had her reasons. "Beats me."

Josie's eyes narrowed. "Unless she wanted me here for a reason. Like to work closely with *you*."

"Why would she care?"

"She's been singing your praises to me for years. Except ever since I moved back here. Since then she hasn't once tried to talk me into throwing myself at you."

"So?"

"It would be just like her to do something this elaborate to get her way."

Trent smiled. "She really thinks we should get together?"

"Don't look so pleased. She also thinks I should seduce cute pizza delivery boys whenever I get the
chance."

"Not even Rafaela could have orchestrated what
you're suggesting."

Josie sipped her coffee, staring out the window over
the kitchen sink. "You're not giving her enough
credit—she's pretty crafty. And we still don't have an
explanation for her odd behavior."

The phone rang, interrupting the conversation. Trent
went to the kitchen wall to answer it.

"Hello?" he said, and he heard his father's greeting
on the other end of the line.

His dad immediately started to complain about how
much trouble women were, and Trent glanced at the
clock. It read ten minutes to ten, and for some reason
that time seemed important. He searched his memory
while his father continued his diatribe, sounding more
frustrated than he had in years.

Trent had hoped Rafaela would turn his father's life
around, but from the sounds of it they weren't even on
speaking terms at the moment. Something about her
telling him he needed to grow up.

The street cleaners! That's what he was supposed to
remember—that his car had to be moved by ten for the
street cleaners.

He covered the mouthpiece on the phone and got
Josie's attention. "Could you please move my car to
the other side of the street for the cleaning truck?" he
whispered.

She nodded, and he took the keys from the wall and
tossed them to her.

It wasn't until he heard the sound of the Porsche's
engine starting that he questioned the sanity of giving

Josie the keys to his car. Even for a drive across the street. But he had to trust that she wouldn't let him down.

A few minutes later she returned in one piece, and he hadn't heard a single metal-against-metal scraping sound, so he assumed there had been no mishaps.

His father was still droning on.

"Dad?" Trent interrupted when he paused for a breath. "I've got company here right now, so I need to let you go. Why don't you come over for dinner tonight?"

After his father agreed and they'd said their goodbyes, Trent hung up the phone and sat back down at the table with Josie.

"That didn't sound good."

"Apparently our parents have had some sort of falling out."

Josie paused midsip and peered at him over the edge of her coffee cup. "You mean, like a lovers' quarrel?"

Trent nodded.

"They're dating seriously?"

"*Were,* I think. Didn't I tell you?"

"*She* never even told me."

"Probably they were just keeping things quiet to avoid upsetting us if it didn't work out."

Josie frowned. "Seems like Mom has been keeping a lot of things from me lately—her coming back from Prague, the possibility of her retirement..."

"Do you have any other job prospects, just in case?"

"Oh, didn't I tell you?" She set her coffee mug down with such force that some of the brown liquid splashed over the rim. "I had an interview Wednesday, and yesterday they offered me a job."

"Who's 'they'?"

"It's a nearby counseling center. They have an opening for a marriage counselor." She smiled, but it looked a little forced.

"Sounds ideal."

"It is. I'd be a fool to turn it down."

"So you accepted the job?"

Her smile disappeared, and her shoulders sagged. "That's the problem. I don't know what's come over me, but when they called, I just couldn't force myself to say yes. I kept thinking about the center, about all the clients there and how I've grown to like so many of them, about how long the place has been in business…"

"It's a San Francisco landmark."

She frowned. "I know. And I just can't imagine it not existing anymore."

Trent puzzled over the facts as he stared at Josie's delicate fingers laced around the coffee mug. Rafaela was no longer interested in running the Lovers for Life Center, but she was the heart and soul of the place.

Since Josie had taken over, though, she'd begun to leave her own mark on the school. He was almost certain the place had taken on a slightly more respectable air in the last couple of months. There were fewer classes with words such as "orgasm" in the title, and more with titles like "Exploring the Sensuality of the Mind" and other such Josie-esque psycho-babble.

He finally said, "She wants to pass the torch on to you."

"I suppose that's it. She's basically said as much."

"You think she was hoping you'd fall in love with running the place while she was in Prague?"

"Probably." The line between her eyebrows appeared again.

"But?"

"But that still doesn't explain why she took all the money in the business account and left me indebted to you."

"Maybe she really was trying to get us together," he said, joking. "Or more likely, it's like you said before, to finance her boyfriend's literary efforts."

"That doesn't make sense, though, the more I think about it. Mom has always been smart about money where her male bimbos are concerned. She doesn't just let them bamboozle her."

She was right, it didn't add up. Had he and Josie fallen right into Rafaela's trap? Were they so predictable that she'd known exactly what would happen if she left Josie with the center and left Trent without his rent payments?

He shook his head. "This is crazy. She couldn't have done all this as some elaborate matchmaking scheme."

Josie shrugged. "I wouldn't put it past her." She turned her gaze to a stack of magazines on the table and began to thumb through the top one.

Trent dug into his now-cold oatmeal, reading the paper as he ate. He became so engrossed in an article about environmental legislation that the sound of Josie's voice again startled him.

"What is this?" she demanded.

Trent glanced up from the paper. His insides twisted into a knot. She was holding up the proposal from MegaBooks. He'd stuck it at the bottom of the stack on the table a few days ago and forgotten about it.

"That's private," he said a little too sharply.

"Did you...*are* you going to sell the two buildings?"

What could he say? That he was considering betraying Rafaela, the neighborhood association that opposed the chain bookstore, Josie herself? Trent stared into his coffee cup, formulating what he hoped would be a benign answer.

"That's just a proposal, not a contract."

"You are going to sell, aren't you?"

He hesitated, and he had no idea why. He wasn't going to sell. Was he? Okay, he'd given it serious thought. But that was only because Josie was showing no sign that she'd changed in the past three years.

She was still the same emotionally distant girl who'd ditched him at the beach. Emotional entanglements sent her running like a scared rabbit. Trent wasn't sure he wanted to stick around, working right next door to her, feeling that stabbing pain in his gut every time they bumped into one another and he was reminded of what might have been.

"I've been thinking for a while now that I might like to run adventure tours full-time."

"You're going to sell Extreme Sports?"

"I could relocate it to Tahoe, or someplace else where tourists go, make it an easier base for the tours."

"What about the Lovers for Life Center?"

"Your lease is coming up for renewal, and Rafaela told me before she went to Prague that she was considering not renewing."

Josie blinked. Whatever she'd been prepared to say got caught in her throat.

"I guess she didn't tell you that?"

"I've been struggling to keep that place afloat all this time…"

"She didn't say if she was closing it. Maybe she just wants to relocate," Trent offered lamely.

Josie glared at the sheet of paper again. "Mega-

Books? You'd really sell to a big chain like that and ruin the individuality of the whole neighborhood?''

Trent had gone over all the negative aspects of the deal in his head a hundred times, and he'd weighed them against the benefits. No matter how he looked at the offer from MegaBooks, it was a lot of money.

"I might, for the right price." It sounded even sleazier spoken out loud than it felt when the idea only occupied his thoughts.

This was free enterprise, right? If the world wanted super-bookstores, who was Trent to stand in the way?

He'd expected Josie to find his comment repulsive, but instead she said, "I guess the kind of money they're offering would be hard to turn down."

"You got it."

"You really want to leave the city?"

"I don't know." *It all depends on you,* he wanted to say but didn't.

That kind of talk was pointless with Josie.

As if to prove his point, she stood up from the table, her expression blank. "I think I should go. I've got a lot of work to do today."

Trent opened his mouth to ask her to stay, but she'd already turned and gone into the bedroom for her clothes. As he listened to the sound of her dressing, running away once again, he knew the best decision would be to sell.

13

JOSIE SWIPED AT THE TEARS that clouded her vision. Damn him, once and for all. She'd had enough of Trent O'Reilly for one lifetime, and she wasn't going to waste another moment believing he was meant to be a part of her life.

She hurried out of the apartment building and down the sidewalk. If he wanted to sell off her dreams, fine. She'd go back to working as a counselor. He could go off to the woods alone and let his money keep him company.

She climbed into her Saab and turned the key in the ignition, but the car's only response was a sickly sputtering, and then silence. Josie tried again. More sputtering, a grinding sound, and then nothing. She tried again. And again. Her poor old car had chosen the worst day possible to kick the bucket.

It had traveled some one hundred and fifty-eight thousand miles for Josie and, judging by the sounds of it, it had decided it wasn't going to go an inch farther—at least not today.

Josie pounded the steering wheel a few times, then leaned her forehead on it and said a silent prayer for what might have been the final passing of the dear old machine.

The day couldn't get much worse. She glared out the window, and her gaze settled on the pristine new bumper of Trent's Porsche. Now there was a car that had plenty of get-up-and-go left in it.

And it was also a car to which she possessed the keys.

An evil idea formed in Josie's head, and the moment it appeared, she knew she would do it.

Digging around in her pocket, she withdrew the keys Trent had given her to move the car for the street cleaner. She'd forgotten to give them back to him, and the right thing to do would be to march back into his apartment that very moment and hand the keys over to the traitorous jerk.

Josie climbed out of her car and locked it. She glanced over at Trent's front window as she went to his car. It only took a moment to unlock it and slip into the driver's seat. The plush leather sports seat alone probably cost what her entire car was worth.

With her hands shaking, she fumbled to get the key into the ignition as she pressed in the clutch. The car started with a low rumble that she prayed Trent wouldn't recognize and come running out to investigate.

Not that he'd have time to catch her. She smiled and pulled out into traffic, her heart pounding. She only intended to drive the car home and park it, then let Trent come and pick it up at his leisure. He would eventually realize she had the keys, after all, so it couldn't be called theft. Not exactly, anyway.

Yet the more she thought about his deception, the more she wanted to do something more than park the car. If only she could inflict a little pain on him, hit him where it hurt the most—in his car. His stupid, male-ego-inflating, overpowered, overpriced piece of German machismo.

But, in her marriage counseling days that was exactly the kind of emotional response she'd counseled angry couples not to have. Stopping with a screech at a red light, she felt the depth of her own naiveté. Back then those couples had always seemed so melodramatic. Now she understood their anger.

Josie took the winding roads through Golden Gate Park, minding the speed limit as best she could with so much horsepower at her disposal. That was when she spotted the tree—a giant live oak they'd once sat beneath in junior high school. It had been on a field trip of some sort; Rafaela had forgotten to pack Josie a lunch and Trent had shared his with her.

A little pang of guilt wedged itself under her rib cage.

Whatever Trent had done to hurt her, she shouldn't be playing so dirty. There was no justification for taking his car. Maybe he hadn't even noticed that it was gone yet. If she took it back now, she might be able to sneak it into its spot unnoticed, then slip away again without a nasty confrontation. Perhaps she could even drop off the keys in the mailbox.

At the next light, Josie turned and headed back toward Trent's apartment. She sped most of the way, hurrying to avoid Trent's wrath. In a couple of minutes she'd made it back to his street.

No police cars, no Trent foaming at the mouth running up and down the street. All looked promising. There was even a spot a few down from where she had originally parked the Porsche.

As Josie slowed, a streak of black fur appeared a few feet in front of the car. She swerved to the left, the opposite direction the cat was heading, her heart pounding in her ears as the animal disappeared from her sight.

Then came the crash, the angry screech of metal against metal, the jarring sensation of being brought to a stop by an immovable object.

Her immovable object.

Beyond the half-crushed hood of the Porsche was the rear left side of her broken-down Saab. She'd crashed right into it. Josie winced at the stress the impact had inflicted on her neck and shoulders but, moving tentatively, she seemed to be fine.

Unlike the cars.

Her fear immediately returned to the cat, though. She looked out at the street. No animal lay there. If she hadn't been mistaken, the streak of black fur had looked a whole lot like Eros.

But that was impossible. He was at the center, over ten blocks away. Whatever animal had run in front of her car was nowhere to be seen. Her stomach lurched at the thought that it might be *under* the car.

She didn't see Trent coming toward her until he was almost at the car. His expression was somewhere between disbelief and outrage. She was done-for.

With shaking hands she opened the car door and stepped out. An apology hovered on her lips, but he didn't give her a chance.

"Are you okay?" he demanded.

"I'm fine." She bent to peer under the Porsche, and her heart started beating again when she knew for sure she hadn't run over the cat.

"Are you *crazy?*" He stopped at his crumpled hood, staring at it as if he'd believed it to be indestructible until now.

"Trent, I'm—"

"You are crazy! That's what this is all about. I should have known to stay the hell away from you. I should have known…"

He shook his head, raked his hands through his hair.

"I'm sorry."

"Should I even ask why you were driving my car?"

"It was stupid. I just wanted to take it for a joyride, and then a cat ran out in front of me and—"

"Oh, now that takes character. Blame your insanity on a defenseless animal."

Josie wasn't sure whether to be more upset about her own car or Trent's. They both looked pretty bad, crunched together in that unnatural position.

Trent pulled a cell phone out of his pocket and dialed a number. A moment later he was reporting the accident to his insurance company, and there was little for Josie to do but to slink back home with her tail between her legs.

She turned and started walking toward home, but she hadn't made it a full block when she heard Trent jogging after her, calling for her to stop.

"Is this about the sale of the building? Does it really make you that angry?"

Fire shot through her belly. She spun around. "Of course it does. You're selling my dream right out from under me."

He stopped short. "I thought you hated that school."

"Maybe I did at one time. But I spent this entire summer putting my heart into it. Do you really think I would have agreed to your stupid lessons if I hadn't been desperate to save the place?" It struck her then just how real her desperation to save the center had been.

Maybe she'd loved the place all along more than she wanted to admit, and maybe it had just been a fear of turning into her mother that kept her from realizing it until now.

"So sleeping with me was an act of desperation."

"Absolutely," she said, then turned and started walking again.

She didn't look back at all, and she prayed he wouldn't follow. She'd made it five blocks before she allowed herself a few tears of self-pity.

It dawned on her halfway home that she was more upset about Trent than she was about closing the center. She'd allowed herself to fall in love with him, when he was clearly still the playboy he'd always been. For him, their lessons had been nothing more than a game. For Josie, they'd been a revelation and an adventure.

How could she call herself an expert on sex when she knew so little about the emotions that inevitably came along with it? How could she have fooled herself into thinking she was worldly enough to keep control of her time with Trent?

It was best that the center close down, because Josie wasn't qualified to run it.

She'd been a fool. Even worse, a romantic fool. Rafaela had always warned her about the dangers of attaching love to sex. She'd preached the importance of self-control, of sensual exploration on a woman's own terms—in spite of her own checkered love life.

Josie wasn't cut out for such coldhearted exploits. She understood now that she didn't want just a great sex life. She wanted love first. She wanted a true, strong love, and she wouldn't settle for the kind of shallow relationships her mother had engaged in so casually for so many years.

She was safely inside her apartment before she broke down into a full-blown crying jag. She headed straight for the kitchen and to the cabinet where she kept her emergency stash of Belgian chocolates, specifically for occasions such as these. The way she felt right now, she'd need the entire stash.

THE INCESSANT RINGING of the telephone woke Josie from a dead sleep. She rolled over and groped across on the nightstand until her hand curled around the phone receiver. Blinking at the glaring red 3:05 on the clock radio, she croaked hello. At this time of night, it could only be her mother calling.

"Josephine? It's Mother. I'm sorry to be calling so late..."

Josie sat bolt upright in bed. Rafaela offering an apology? Something had to be wrong.

"What? What is it?"

"Tony and I have gotten into a bit of a bind. We're at the police station."

"Are you okay?" Josie demanded, her heart waking up and pounding as images of a late-night mugging—or worse—flashed in her head.

"We've been booked, and now they're letting us go. But they want a family member to come get us."

"You've been what?" But she'd heard just fine. Her brain needed to hear again what her mother had just said to believe it.

"Booked, dear. We've been arrested and charged with committing indecent exposure, or some such nonsense, and...performing a lewd act in a public place, I believe is what they said."

Oh. God. Why couldn't her mother be like other middle-aged moms? Maybe join a book club or a quilting circle instead of spending her free time performing lewd acts in public.

"But...I thought you two were no longer on speaking terms."

"Oh, we made up tonight. Boy did we ever make up."

"Say no more. I'd like to be spared the details."

"Fine, just come get me."

"Which police station?" Josie asked as she turned on a lamp.

"We're downtown."

She muttered a reassurance that she'd be there as soon as she could and hung up the phone. She hopped out of bed and shuffled to the closet to pull out a pair of jeans and a shirt, appropriate attire, she guessed, for bailing one's mother out of jail in the middle of the night.

She slid her feet into shoes and headed for the door, smiling as she thought of how she would tell this story to Trent later. But the smile faded from her lips as she remembered that she and Trent were no longer speaking. And then, even worse, her groggy brain finally realized that Trent had probably just received a similar call from his father and would also be headed for the police station.

She might even see him there. Grabbing her keys and purse next to the door, she couldn't resist the urge to glance into the hallway mirror to straighten her bed-head hairdo a bit. But no more than that. She wasn't out to impress Trent, after all. She couldn't care less what he thought.

She hadn't seen him in the week since she'd wrecked his car. He'd dropped off a letter at the center stating the extent of the damages and the cost for repairs, but he'd left it with Erika. Josie was still waiting for official notice that the center would be losing its lease, but in the meantime, she'd alerted Erika to the fact that she ought to start looking for a new job. Josie had arranged to start work at the counseling center as soon as her work at Lovers for Life was finished.

Her own car had mysteriously started just fine the next time she tried it. The rear right corner was still crunched from her wreck, but she'd managed to pry the metal back away from the wheel enough with a crow bar that the car could be driven. As soon as she saved up enough money, she'd have the poor old girl repaired.

Josie navigated the near-empty streets of the city, her stomach in knots over thoughts of Trent. She simply had to get over him. There was no other choice.

Twenty minutes later she found a parking spot in front of the downtown police precinct and then hurried into the building.

It was easy to spot Trent, since he was ten feet ahead of her entering the building, the only other person present besides a police officer at the counter, a scantily clad woman of dubious employment and a scruffy man in a filthy orange raincoat. Trent turned and caught her watching him.

His expression darkened momentarily. He forced a smile and shrugged. "Parents—what're you gonna do?"

Josie smiled in spite of herself. "Murder them?"

The police officer at the counter gave her an odd look, and she blushed.

"I'm joking," she assured him.

He grunted and turned his attention back to his paperwork.

"I'm here to pick up Rafaela Marcus," she said, and he nodded without looking up.

"And I'm here for Anthony O'Reilly."

Josie looked at Trent and shrugged. "Guess we'd better have a seat, huh? I wonder why they aren't out here.''

"Maybe they had to lock them in separate cells to keep them from performing any more lewd acts in public.'' His voice dripped sarcasm, but Josie could tell by his half smile that he approved of their parents being together.

Josie smiled, feeling all the tension drain from her shoulders. Trent had that effect on her. She realized in that instant that she missed his jokes. Even at a police station in the middle of the night, he seemed at ease.

She, on the other hand, was still in shock. Her mother hadn't even acknowledged to Josie that she was having a relationship with Anthony until now. She supposed, if they were happy together, it would be good for both of them.

Trent stared at her. "You look nice, for four in the morning.''

"Thanks, so do you.''

Their gazes locked and an awkward silence fell between them. Moments later it was broken by the sound of footsteps and Rafaela's voice in the hallway.

"I'm sure your wife would love my seminars, Officer Malcolm. They'll make a nice birthday gift.''

Her mother never missed the opportunity to improve someone's sex life, not even if that someone had just arrested her, apparently.

Josie and Trent exchanged an exasperated look when their bedraggled parents appeared in the lobby, escorted by Officer Malcolm.

"You two promise to behave yourselves from now on? No more hanky-panky in public?''

"Of course, dear. We just got a little carried away. I promise it won't happen again.''

"These your escorts?" The officer nodded toward Josie and Trent.

"Yes, these are our children," Rafaela answered.

He looked at Josie. "Keep them out of trouble." The officer shook his head and disappeared back down the hallway, leaving the two errant parents to be dealt with by their reluctant offspring.

Anthony smiled and shrugged at Josie and Trent. "Sorry to drag you two into this mess, but if you don't mind, I think Rafaela and I would like to go home on our own. Can we borrow one of your cars?"

This was a development Josie hadn't anticipated. Apparently not even being arrested could tame their parents' out-of-control libidos. Anthony and Rafaela were gazing at each other like lovesick teenagers. They seemed oblivious to the sterile surroundings and the uncomfortable presence of their adult children.

She saw now that they weren't just in lust, they were in love. And when she turned her gaze from them to Trent, she understood just how badly she wanted the same for herself and him. Perhaps it was too late for them now. She'd made mistakes. She'd been afraid to trust. She hadn't even given them a chance.

And now she was paying a dear price.

Since neither of them volunteered to give up a vehicle, Trent's father persisted.

"Trent, can we take your car? I'm sure Josie wouldn't mind giving you a ride home," he said.

And Josie knew in that moment, this was her last chance to do what she should have done three years ago. Regardless of whether he was selling the buildings, moving to Tahoe—whatever. She had to try at least once.

"Yes, let me give you a ride," she said to Trent.

He nodded. To their parents he said, "No hanky-panky in my SUV. Understand?"

Rafaela waved a hand of dismissal. "We wouldn't dream of it."

Five minutes later Josie sat in the driver's seat, an eery sense of déjà vu hanging between herself and Trent. One of the last times they'd been in her beat-up old car together, their relationship had hit rock-bottom.

Trent cleared his throat, breaking the silence, then muttered, "Can you believe those two?"

Josie made a right turn away from the route to Trent's neighborhood, hoping he wouldn't notice.

"I can believe the arrest and the charges, but I'm a little shocked to see my mother so head-over-heels in love, and with a guy her age to boot."

"I've got a feeling this was some kind of setup to get us together again. Whadda you think?"

Josie blinked at the idea. Interesting. And not out of her mother's range of creativity. "Hmm," she said, mulling over the possibilities.

For the first time in her life she was getting the feeling that her mother really did know best. And as unconventional as Rafaela was, maybe she did have her ways of making sure Josie's life headed in the right direction.

"Where are you going?"

She glanced over at him and offered a shaky smile. "I hope you don't mind being kidnapped. We need to talk."

"About?"

"Unfinished business. I promise I'll take you straight home after."

"Guess I don't have any choice."

She smiled more confidently then. "I knew you'd see

it my way. I'm truly sorry about your car, by the way. I'll pay for all the damage, I promise.''

''No hurry,'' he said quietly. ''I've been meaning to tell you, anyway, that I decided not to sell the buildings. The center is free to renew its lease for as long as you want.''

Josie smiled at the good news, but she understood now that keeping the center running wasn't nearly as important as tending to her sadly neglected personal life.

Josie pulled her car into the very same spot where they'd parked more than three years ago, overlooking Ocean Beach. It was dark, but they could hear the waves crashing close by.

This might very well be their last night together, but she couldn't dwell on that. She believed it was their destiny to come together here, at least once more, for one unforgettable night. She would always have this night to remember when she was old and gray and living alone.

''I owe you,'' she said.

''Like I said, no hurry on the car.''

''No, for three years ago, I owe you.''

Trent smiled. He understood. ''Josie, I appreciate the gesture, but I've forgiven you. We don't have to—''

She leaned over and kissed him, soft and deep.

''I made a big mistake, Trent. I never gave us a chance.''

''No, you didn't.'' His gaze was penetrating, even in the dark.

''I want to now, if it's not too late. I didn't realize until you were gone that...'' She paused, savoring the truth, that she was head over heals, hopelessly in love with Trent.

"That what?"

"I love you."

He took her hands in his now and pulled her close. He kissed her very gently, as if he were asking a question.

"Don't you want to know what your payment is?" Josie asked.

"Payment for what?"

"For years of unrequited lust and unconsummated encounters."

"Oh, *that*. We have kind of made up for it lately, don't you think?" He grinned. "So what's my payment?"

"Sex on the beach, of course."

Trent leaned his head back on the seat and sighed. "Sorry, babe, that's not good enough."

"But—" Her heart dropped to her belly.

"That's what I wanted three years ago, and even a few months ago, but it's not what I want now."

Josie felt her stomach curl up into a little ball around her fallen heart. She'd let her fears rule her for too long and now she was going to lose the best thing in her life because of it.

"I'm sorry, I just thought…"

"I want you," he said.

Huh? She did a double take. He was looking at her, dead serious, his eyes filled with the emotion she'd seen in them the last time they'd made love. "You want me?"

"And not just for one night, or for two hours a week, or for two months. I want you, all the time, forever."

Josie blinked back tears. "That's a lot of sex on the beach."

"Damn right it is." He grinned, leaned over, and

pulled her into his arms. Kissed her again. Pulled her shirt up and slid his hands underneath. "I just have one question."

"Hmm?" She nuzzled her face into his neck, intoxicating herself with his scent, and planted a soft kiss there.

"Whatever happened to my boxers?"

"Oh, the ones I drove away with?" She leaned forward and opened the glove compartment. "They're right here."

Trent spotted the blue paisley fabric and looked over at Josie. "You kept them in your glove box for three years?"

"I guess I've always hoped I'd get a chance to give them back to you."

He smiled, then pulled her into his arms again.

He was the one—the perfect lover and companion she'd hardly dared to wish for. She'd been so afraid of not finding him she'd run away before she ever got the chance. But Trent hadn't let her run away this time. And she was thankful. Oh, so thankful.

Epilogue

Three Months Later...

RAFAELA LOVED SITTING in the waiting areas of airports, watching people say their goodbyes, and even better, watching them greet arriving loved ones. The hugging, the kissing, the happy bursts of conversation—it was all enough to make even her skeptical old heart swell.

She turned her attention from the window, where she'd been watching for the plane to arrive, to Anthony, who was browsing a nearby newsstand. Who would have guessed she'd finally find the love of her life after all these years? Not her. Truth be told, she'd all but given up on the idea before she'd met Anthony again.

They'd known each other years ago, yes, and maybe there'd been some sparks that they'd ignored out of respect to his marriage. But the moment she'd laid eyes on him in that restaurant, she'd known in her heart she'd found a long-lost jewel from her past.

She caught herself twirling the ring on her left hand again. The ruby ring was a tad big, but she hadn't been able to part with it to have it sized ever since Anthony had given it to her two months ago. Besides, she'd been so busy helping plan her daughter's wedding, and now her own next month...

Rafaela blinked back a tear as she saw the plane land

in the distance. Trent and Josie were coming back from their honeymoon of hiking in Hawaii.

Anthony slipped into the chair next to her, and Rafaela discretely wiped away the moisture in her eye.

"Is that their plane?"

"I think so." She looked at him and frowned. "Do you think I should let them call me Grandma?"

"You don't look like a grandma to me," he said, waggling his eyebrows and giving her knee a squeeze.

"I can't get over how happy Josie was on the phone last night." The fact that she'd even called Rafaela as soon as she had the home pregnancy test results was…remarkable.

"Seems like you two are finally getting along like a mother and daughter should."

She sighed. "It's about time."

"Not many moms would go to all the trouble you have to make sure their girl is happy."

"Maybe not." But no one had ever accused Rafaela of being like other moms.

She stood to watch as passengers from the arriving flight came filing out the door of the gate. When she spotted Josie and Trent, hand in hand, she smiled at the evidence of her hard work coming to fruition.

It hadn't been easy getting Josie and Trent together, but they were well worth the trouble.

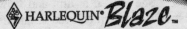

HARLEQUIN® Blaze™

GUESS WHO'S STEAMING UP THESE SHEETS...?

It's talented Blaze author Kristin Hardy!
With a hot new miniseries:

Watch for the following titles and keep an eye out for a
special bed that brings a special night to each of these
three incredible couples!

#78 SCORING March 2003
Becka Landon and Mace Duvall know how the *game* is played,
they just can't agree on who seduced whom *first!*

#86 AS BAD AS CAN BE May 2003
Mallory Carson and Shay O'Connor are rivals in the bar business—
but *never* in the bedroom....

#94 SLIPPERY WHEN WET July 2003
Taylor DeWitt and Beckett Stratford *accidentally* find themselves
on the honeymoon of a lifetime!

*Don't miss this trilogy of sexy stories...
Available wherever Harlequin books are sold.*

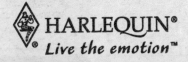

HARLEQUIN®
Live the emotion™

Visit us at www.eHarlequin.com

HBBTS

USA TODAY *bestselling author*

JULIE KENNER

Brings you a supersexy tale of love and mystery...

Silent ~~CONF~~ESSIONS

A BRAND-NEW NOVEL.

Detective Jack Parker needs an education from a historical sex expert in order to crack his latest case—and bookstore owner Veronica Archer is just the person to help him. But their private lessons give Ronnie some other ideas on how the detective can help *her* sexual education....

"JULIE KENNER JUST MIGHT WELL BE THE MOST ENCHANTING AUTHOR IN TODAY'S MARKET."
—THE ROMANCE READER'S CONNECTION

Look for SILENT CONFESSIONS, available in April 2003.

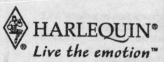

HARLEQUIN®
Live the emotion™

Visit us at www.eHarlequin.com

PHSC

If you enjoyed what you just read,
then we've got an offer you can't resist!

Take 2 bestselling love stories FREE!

Plus get a FREE surprise gift!

Clip this page and mail it to Harlequin Reader Service®

IN U.S.A.	IN CANADA
3010 Walden Ave.	P.O. Box 609
P.O. Box 1867	Fort Erie, Ontario
Buffalo, N.Y. 14240-1867	L2A 5X3

YES! Please send me 2 free Blaze™ novels and my free surprise gift. After receiving them, if I don't wish to receive anymore, I can return the shipping statement marked cancel. If I don't cancel, I will receive 4 brand-new novels each month, before they're available in stores! In the U.S.A., bill me at the bargain price of $3.80 plus 25¢ shipping and handling per book and applicable sales tax, if any*. In Canada, bill me at the bargain price of $4.21 plus 25¢ shipping and handling per book and applicable taxes**. That's the complete price and a savings of at least 10% off the cover prices—what a great deal! I understand that accepting the 2 free books and gift places me under no obligation ever to buy any books. I can always return a shipment and cancel at any time. Even if I never buy another book from Harlequin, the 2 free books and gift are mine to keep forever.

150 HDN DNWD
350 HDN DNWE

Name	(PLEASE PRINT)	
Address	Apt.#	
City	State/Prov.	Zip/Postal Code

* Terms and prices subject to change without notice. Sales tax applicable in N.Y.
** Canadian residents will be charged applicable provincial taxes and GST.
   All orders subject to approval. Offer limited to one per household and not valid to current Blaze™ subscribers.
   ® are registered trademarks of Harlequin Enterprises Limited.

BLZ02-R

eHARLEQUIN.com

Becoming an eHarlequin.com member is easy,
fun and **FREE!** Join today to enjoy great benefits:

- **Super savings** on all our books, including
  members-only discounts and offers!

- Enjoy **exclusive online reads—FREE!**

- Info, tips and **expert advice** on writing
  your own romance novel.

- FREE romance **newsletters,**
  customized by you!

- Find out the latest on your
  favorite authors.

- Enter to win exciting **contests
  and promotions!**

- Chat with other members in our
  community message boards!

Plus, we'll send you 2 FREE Internet-exclusive
eHarlequin.com books (no strings!)
just to say thanks for joining us online.

To become a member,
visit www.eHarlequin.com today!

INTMEMB

A "Mother of the Year" contest brings
overwhelming response as thousands of women
vie for the luxurious grand prize....

Kate Hoffmann

Jacqueline Diamond

Jill Shalvis

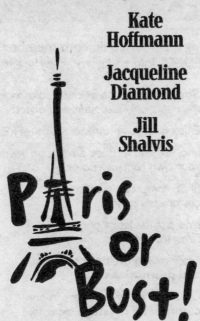

Paris or Bust!

A hilarious and romantic trio of new stories!

With a trip to Paris at stake, these women are
determined to win! But the laughs are many as three of
them discover that being finalists isn't the most
excitement they'll ever have.... Falling in love is!

Available in April 2003.

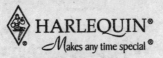

HARLEQUIN®

Makes any time special ®

Visit us at www.eHarlequin.com

PHPOB

There's nothing sexier than a man in uniform...
so just imagine what three will be like!

MEN OF COURAGE

**A brand-new anthology from
USA TODAY bestselling author**

LORI
FOSTER

DONNA
KAUFFMAN

JILL
SHALVIS

**These heroes are strong, fearless...
and absolutely impossible to resist!**

Look for MEN OF COURAGE in May 2003!

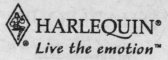

HARLEQUIN®
Live the emotion™

Visit us at www.eHarlequin.com

PHMOC

AMERICAN HEROES

These men are heroes— strong, fearless... And impossible to resist!

Join bestselling authors Lori Foster, Donna Kauffman
and Jill Shalvis as they deliver up

MEN OF COURAGE

Harlequin anthology
May 2003

Followed by *American Heroes* miniseries
in Harlequin Temptation

RILEY by Lori Foster
June 2003

SEAN by Donna Kauffman
July 2003

LUKE by Jill Shalvis
August 2003

Don't miss this sexy new miniseries by some of
Temptation's hottest authors!

Available at your favorite retail outlet.

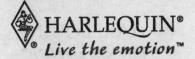

Live the emotion™

Visit us at www.eHarlequin.com

HTAH